Canberraesque

Robert Phillips

First published by Busybird Publishing 2017

Copyright © 2017 Robert Phillips

ISBN 978-1-925585-96-4

This book is copyright. Apart from any fair dealing for the purposes of study, research, criticism, review, or as otherwise permitted under the Copyright Act, no part may be reproduced by any process without written permission. Enquiries should be made through the publisher. The characters in this story are fictitious. Any similarity to any person, living or historical, is purely coincidental.

Cover image: Phil Kavanagh
Layout and typesetting: Busybird Publishing
Editor: Terrri Giuretis
Artist: Phil Kavanagh

Busybird Publishing
2/118 Para Road
Montmorency, Victoria
Australia 3094
www.busybird.com.au

Contents

Part One
Crispin Spalding

1. The Snows of Yesteryear

1 January 2101

On the mast at the summit of Parliament House, the big Australian flag hung limply. With the first hush of the morning breeze, it stirred into life, shaking a fine layer of dust from its faded fabric as it unfurled.

President Crispin Spalding stepped outside, blinked his eyes to accustom to the harsh sunlight, and stared out to the west. He was a tall, balding man with a robust frame but a face that was weather-beaten by six decades in a harsh climate.

He took a slow, deep breath as he prepared to face the day's calamities. The first struck him immediately – a coughing fit caused by the fine dust spilling from the flag.

It would be another scorching day, with the temperature climbing to over 40 degrees. The westerly wind was picking up: already he could see the dust clouds rolling in over the cheerless brown slopes of the Brindabella Ranges.

Cheerless was how he felt, in a world of relentless heat, drought and dust storms. 'But where,' he lamented, 'are the snows of yesteryear?'

***

In a warming world, the snows of Crispin Spalding's yesteryears had been few. He was born in the Canberra Region in 2040, when the Brindabellas were seldom speckled with white.

He was seven when a rare event happened that would leave an imprint on his memories for the rest of his long life. A freak cold snap meant that the snow cover on the Brindabellas was substantial. His parents took him up there to experience the thrill of slithering around on the icy drifts and the fun of a snowball fight.

It was the only time he set foot on snow. Within a few years, he would never see its like again.

The shy, slim, fair-haired lad of seven would grow up to become a big-framed man of robust build. He radiated an aura of strength and energy, and above all, of self-confidence. Because he wanted to become a foreign correspondent and visit strange, faraway lands, he enrolled for a degree in media studies.

His dream was soon shattered: there were no longer any foreign correspondents, because the foreign content of news was declining. A world of ten billion people had reached its limits, and Gaia, the Earth Goddess was wreaking her revenge. Overpopulation, resource shortages, financial crises, global warming and other environmental damage were taking their toll. Disaster followed disaster until people switched off: the chaos of the rest of the world was just too much. Australians had enough problems of their own. Our economy hadn't actually collapsed, but it was looking rickety.

Crispin's one consolation was that he met Maya. She was pretty in a cute way with mischievous eyes that revealed her inner pixie.

'Maya is an unusual name,' he told her.

'It's a family tradition. My mother's name is Maya.'

'And her mother?'

'Is called Christine. She went to a wild end-of-the-world party in December 2012.'

'Was that something to do with the Mayan calendar?'

Maya nodded. 'Of course, the world didn't end. So, nine months later, when she gave birth to mum, she named her Maya.'

When they graduated, Crispin and Maya got married. He became a political journalist and she a publicist with the CSIRO. They would have a son and a daughter who bore their names.

Politics fascinated Crispin. Australia was then a republic of over 30 million that had replaced its obsolete collection of state, territory and local governments with a network of regional administrations.

He discovered that with his imposing stature, his confidence, and his clear, succinct manner of speech, he was an impressive public speaker. In his mid-twenties he successfully stood as a candidate for the Canberra Regional Assembly.

It wasn't long before the nuts and bolts of regional politics, of street realignments, blocked drains and planning enquiries bored him. By his early thirties, he was elected to the Australian Parliament. He had no idea, when he first walked into 'the House on the Hill' that his involvement with it would last for decades.

He made rousing speeches about the need to turn around Australia's economy, which was steadily declining in real terms by several per cent per annum. Maya asked him how the rest of the world was performing.

'Most economies are declining by at least twice as much as ours. But that isn't the point. Our standard of living will be halved in less than twenty years if we keep going as we are now.'

***

One evening, Maya's boss came to dinner. Dr Norman Tweed was known as the Chief Geek, because he was the new head of the CSIRO. He was an annoyingly cheerful fellow who had been through university at the same time as Maya and Crispin. Most annoying of all, he had dark curly hair while Crispin's hairline was receding so much that people were calling him 'Spalding the Balding.'

They tried to avoid talking about politics over dinner, but once Crispin got onto his favourite topic, it was hard to shut him up.

'Ignore him,' said Maya. 'He's just trying to ruin our digestion.'

Norman laughed. 'I've heard it all before.'

'Aren't you worried about our country's future?' asked Crispin indignantly.

'Yes. But look, what's happening to the human race is what happens to most species. Their numbers increase until they reach the limits of what their environment can sustain. In favourable circumstances, they'll build up to plague proportions, like mice or locusts or humans.'

'You're saying that we're a plague?'

'More or less. The damage we've done to the world is like a plague.' Norman ruffled his curly hair. 'Only, whereas with most plagues, the numbers build up and die off within months, we've built up our numbers over centuries, and we'll die off over decades.'

'Die off?' Maya looked at their little ones, who were toying with their greens. 'How much?'

Norman looked briefly up, as if staring at the ceiling. 'At a rough guess, world population will fall to a few hundred million. Maybe a billion, depending on how much technology we keep.'

'And Australia?' asked Crispin warily.

'If we revert to a pre-industrial society, perhaps the same as before European settlement - a few hundred thousand. Life expectancy would drop to thirty or forty.

'If we can keep some of our technology, despite our limited resources, maybe we'll have a society like we had at Federation: three or four millions with a life expectancy of fifty or sixty.'

The Spaldings were quiet for a moment, while they took all of this in. 'You know the most important thing we've learnt from three hundred years of civilisation?'

'What's that?' asked Maya.

'Personal hygiene.' Norman stared at the children. 'Always wash your hands before meals, and you should live to be at least fifty.'

'Fifty is old,' retorted little Maya.

Norman laughed. 'In times to come, it probably will be.'

***

Maya was so concerned by what Norman told them that she became a devout Gaian. She believed, as many people would do, that climate change was Gaia's Curse. The Earth goddess was punishing people for the way they had mistreated her planet.

Crispin, meanwhile, became the Minister of Communications. It was a thankless job: the broadband cables and wireless transmitters were breaking down, and the satellite network was not being maintained. Data transmission rates were becoming as slow as they had been in the ancient dial-up days.

Australia's media networks were in chaos. Even the ABC was struggling to maintain its networks because of shortages of government funding.

In 2078, Crispin arranged a conference of media owners to sort out the mess. He decided that the best answer was rationalisation. 'What I want to see in each region,' he proposed, 'are two TV and two radio stations, one ABC and one commercial, and one online newspaper with a mixture of national and regional news.'

So the ABC had to rationalise its operations, while the muddle of commercial media pooled their resources to set up a network of regional stations and newspapers. It was a minimalist approach, but at least it meant that basic media services were provided.

He realised that news was becoming increasingly regional. Having given up on the world, people were now losing interest in what was happening in the rest of Australia.

This gave him a brainwave. In 2080, Crispin Spalding decided to run for President, campaigning on the issue of giving the regional governments more power. 'Hand the government back to the people' was his slogan. His opponents argued that this would be an abrogation of power by the Australian Government, and would lead to the disintegration of the nation.

The election campaign was exciting – the primaries, the whistle-stop tours, the television debates with his main rival, and, of course, election night itself and the cliff-hanger result in his favour.

During his first term as President, the Australian Government handed most of its powers and revenue sources to the regions. Government departments in Canberra were reduced to a series of directorates, ostensively co-ordinating the activities of the regions.

The regions soon realised that they had been handed the poison chalice: more responsibility for schools, health care, roads and social security, but steadily declining revenue. The Australian Government had abrogated its power, and the nation was disintegrating.

Everybody blamed Crispin Spalding for anything that went wrong. They knew it wasn't really his fault, that the problems had started much earlier in that ill-fated century. They had to blame someone, and being the President, the buck stopped with him. Yet he tried his best, so people re-elected him. Besides, it was clear that no-one else really wanted the job.

At the time, Australia was in the grip of a twenty-year drought. The scorching winds and the dust storms turned the neighbouring region of Riverina into a dustbowl. The Murray-Darling river system became a series of water holes. Bushfires were so fierce that all the authorities could do was to evacuate everyone who was in their paths, and let great swathes of countryside burn.

In 2088, Australia's tricentenary year, there was a brief resurgence of national pride. President Spalding capitalised on it long enough to be elected for a third term, although by then, even he was beginning to wonder why he bothered. Sessions of parliament were becoming shorter and shorter. Why go to Canberra when the Australian Government was running out of money?

By 2092, at the end of his third term, Crispin Spalding was ready to throw in the towel. The Electoral Office said it could scrape together enough money to hold the elections, providing that the regional administrations ran most of it from their end.

It was then that nature intervened. The drought was broken with a vengeance. There were torrential rains, catastrophic floods, and raging seas that battered the coastlines. Worst of all, as predicted by climate scientists, cyclones had been pushing further southwards: Cyclone Beelzebub wreaked havoc upon Sydney.

The elections were postponed because the Australian government had to put much of its meagre resources into helping Sydney recover. It was agreed that President Spalding and the other elected representatives would stay in office *pro tem*, until economic conditions improved enough for the elections to be held.

But things did not improve. Even when the drought returned, the coasts continued to be battered by the rising waters. Eight years later, the elections had still not been held, and the slopes of the Brindabellas were an unrelenting brown.

2. Prophecy

Crispin Spalding went back inside, to wander among the dusty, deserted corridors of power. He walked into the House of Representatives chamber. Once the scene of passion and debate, its seats were now coated in a layer of the fine dust that got into everything.

If his face had not been so dried by the hot winds, he might have shed a tear: today, of all days, the Members and Senators should be here. The first of January 2101 was the bicentenary of Federation – the 200th anniversary of the day that Australia became a nation. He had sent them an email suggesting they all gather in Canberra for this special event. One or two replied that it would be kind of nice to have some sort of function, but they were too busy with local matters to attend. Most didn't even bother to respond.

As he stood by the Speaker's chair, he made a decision. Whether borne of frustration by the sheer indifference of the politicians, or simply in a fit of pique, President Crispin Spalding would send out an email to announce to the people of Australia that he was suspending the Constitution, dissolving the Australian Parliament, and making himself President For Life.

***

He had hoped to shock the erstwhile MPs into taking an interest. All he got were five emails saying things like 'it was a bit of a shame' or 'yeah, whatever'. He soon realised that he had given himself a life sentence.

At least Canberrans had clung to a shred of pride by insisting that he was still 'Mr President' even though they were no longer sure what he was president of. President of Canberra, maybe. It still existed as a coherent entity, and had expanded its domain to include Queanbeyan and other neighbouring towns.

By 2101, Canberrans' main preoccupation was the arrival of more Dirt People. These hapless folk had started coming in from the Hay Plains about twenty years earlier, leaving their properties to turn into even bigger dust bowls than they were already. Now, the people of the inland towns were on the move. Young, Griffith and Orange had already been swallowed up by the desert, while drifts of sand slid eerily around the deserted streets of Wagga.

Canberra had become the Mecca for the Dirt People because of the once mighty Cotter Dam. True, it was now only at 20% capacity, but it was still the biggest water hole for hundreds of kilometres around.

The trouble was, Canberra was struggling to support the people it already had. Crispin tried to turn some of the refugees away. He attempted the Yass solution and the Goulburn solution, but the Dirt People kept coming. In desperation, he turned to the Lake George solution. There was water underneath the crusted flats of what had once been a lake bed. He ordered the setting up of tent villages on the western side of the lake.

But there were soon tents springing up on the eastern side of Lake George as well. Because of rising sea levels, people were trekking inland from the coastal regions. They became known, after a band of invaders in the ancient world, as the Sea People.

Already, half of Sydney was being intermittently flooded, while many of the coastal towns were falling into the sea. The Sea People had swarmed into the Blue Mountains, and were now spilling out onto the plains.

The tented villages on Lake George grew larger and larger, and moved in from both sides until they met in the middle. There were violent scenes as both sides wrestled for control of the lake bed's vital but diminishing water supplies.

The Dirt People and the Sea People were in their tents one night when there was a storm. It seldom rained, but when it did, there were the violent downpours characteristic of desert regions. A great wall of water swept into Lake George and filled it to a depth of at least two metres. Many of the people were drowned. The survivors from both sides hauled themselves out of the mud, joined forces and made for Canberra. They called themselves the Mud People.

***

Another decade went by. President Spalding clung to power for three reasons:

i.   the Canberra Regional Assembly, which was supposed to be running the regional government, had become virtually defunct due to lack of funding;

ii. as long as he was 'Mr President', people felt that somebody was in charge, even if they weren't sure what he was in charge of; and

iii. having been in power for so long, he couldn't think what else he could do with his time.

The droughts continued, interspersed with occasional heavy downpours. At least, the refugees had stopped coming. The Mud People had been housed at the showgrounds of EPIC in temporary accommodation (in which they would live for generations). The remaining Dirt People had all dispersed from the Riverina to Canberra and other places. News from outside Canberra was now sparse, but there were reports that the Sea People had been stopped in a series of battles in the Blue Mountains.

Speaking of news, the television stations had broken down. One local radio station was still operating, on low power, and run mainly by community volunteers. Many of the receivers were now crystal sets. There was one weekly newspaper, now produced in hard copy because internet services were breaking down. It wasn't very big because even recycled paper was in short supply.

Because the inter-regional transport systems had largely disintegrated, Canberrans were forced to grow their own food. Much of the open ground was being turned into a mixture of government, private and community owned farms and vegetable gardens.

With government and private wealth declining, most of it was in community hands. President Spalding wondered whether the changes in control of the production of wealth would eventually be reflected in the political and social superstructure.

One person who remained cheerful throughout this time was the Chief Geek, Dr Norman Tweed. 'Running true to form, the human race may have just managed in the nick of time to prevent global warming from going critical. As far as we can tell from the limited data we are receiving, CO_2 levels and temperatures may be starting to stabilise.'

'I guess that's good news,' said Crispin.

'Well, it's not bad news. It means that the climate may not get that much worse. But it will be centuries before things start to improve.'

'Oh.' Crispin frowned. Truth to tell, he was a troubled man. He had recently reached the proverbial three score and ten, and he was contemplating his place in history.

What had he achieved in nearly fifty years of political life? The best that could be said was that he had managed the strategic withdrawal of government as its resources had dried up, like much of the nation.

Was there one thing he could be remembered for? One thing, where people in future generations would say, 'Crispin Spalding? Yes, he made a difference.'

It was Maya who gave him the idea. Her salary having ceased long ago, she had continued as a volunteer at the CSIRO. 'They're still doing good work, you know – taking weather readings, trying out techniques of dry land farming, running seminars.'

'That's it!' Crispin gave her a hug. 'That's one thing I can do.'

He got together with Dr Tweed and the Vice-Chancellor of the Australian National University to devise a plan for the survival of the CSIRO and the ANU. Located next to each other, they were two sides of the same coin. One would be the guardian of scientific and technical knowledge, while the other would preserve the social sciences and the arts.

Exercising his reserve powers as President, Crispin Spalding expropriated lands and the last of the regional government's meagre funds. He set up the Black Mountain Trust to be run jointly by the two institutions. It would give them enough resources to be self-sustaining. They would supplement their incomes by giving technical advice to farmers.

From amongst the school students (most of whom now did not go beyond primary school) the Trust would select the brightest to continue their education. A few would join the siblinghood of the CSIRO and the ANU, to perpetuate the tribe of scholars.

Thus would the knowledge of the race be preserved, in expectation of the time when things would improve sufficiently that civilisation could be rebuilt. This would be the legacy of Crispin Spalding.

***

When he was an old man, Crispin Spalding was taken by his friends and relations up to the Mount Ainslie Lookout. He was past eighty, and his once robust frame was now frail. His face was sad and careworn: a few years earlier, he had buried his beloved Maya, a victim of heat stroke in a warming world.

'I have lived beyond my time,' he sadly told his children and grandchildren.

Staring out across the dusty suburbs towards the drying up lakebed of Burley-Griffin, he contemplated what his time had brought. As Gaia's Curse descended upon the world, and the economy disintegrated, people had to organise themselves into local communities in order to survive. They had lost interest in world politics, then national politics, and now even regional politics. Their mindset had become 'think locally, act locally'.

The residents of North Lyneham had pooled their resources and formed a suburban co-operative. Having a sense of humour, they declared their enclave to be the Grand Duchy of North Lyneham. They called the chairperson of their enterprise the Grand Duke.

It was all a bit of harmless fun, or so it seemed at the time. The North Lynehamites said they had 'mock delusions of grandeur'. In the torrid and torpid days of the 22nd century, the laconic Aussie sense of humour was important for people's sanity.

Then, that venerable institution, the Downer Community Association, declared its suburb to be a Duchy, and its convenor a Duchess. Other suburbs soon followed, while Queanbeyan elected its own queen.

Truth to tell, it did reflect an underlying reality. People were already reluctant to venture into each other's communities, while strangers visiting theirs were viewed with unease. In Crispin Spalding's life time, the focus of the human mind had contracted from the world to the nation, the region, and finally, the local community.

He fixed his gaze on the brown range of hills in the distance. He thought back to that magical day when he was seven years old and his father had taken him to play in the snow. It brought a tear to his eye.

Turning to his loved ones, he uttered what became known as Crispin's Prophecy: 'when next you see snow on the Brindabellas, you will know that Gaia's Curse is being lifted.'

Part Two
Crispin VII

Districts of the Canberra Region (circa 23rd century)

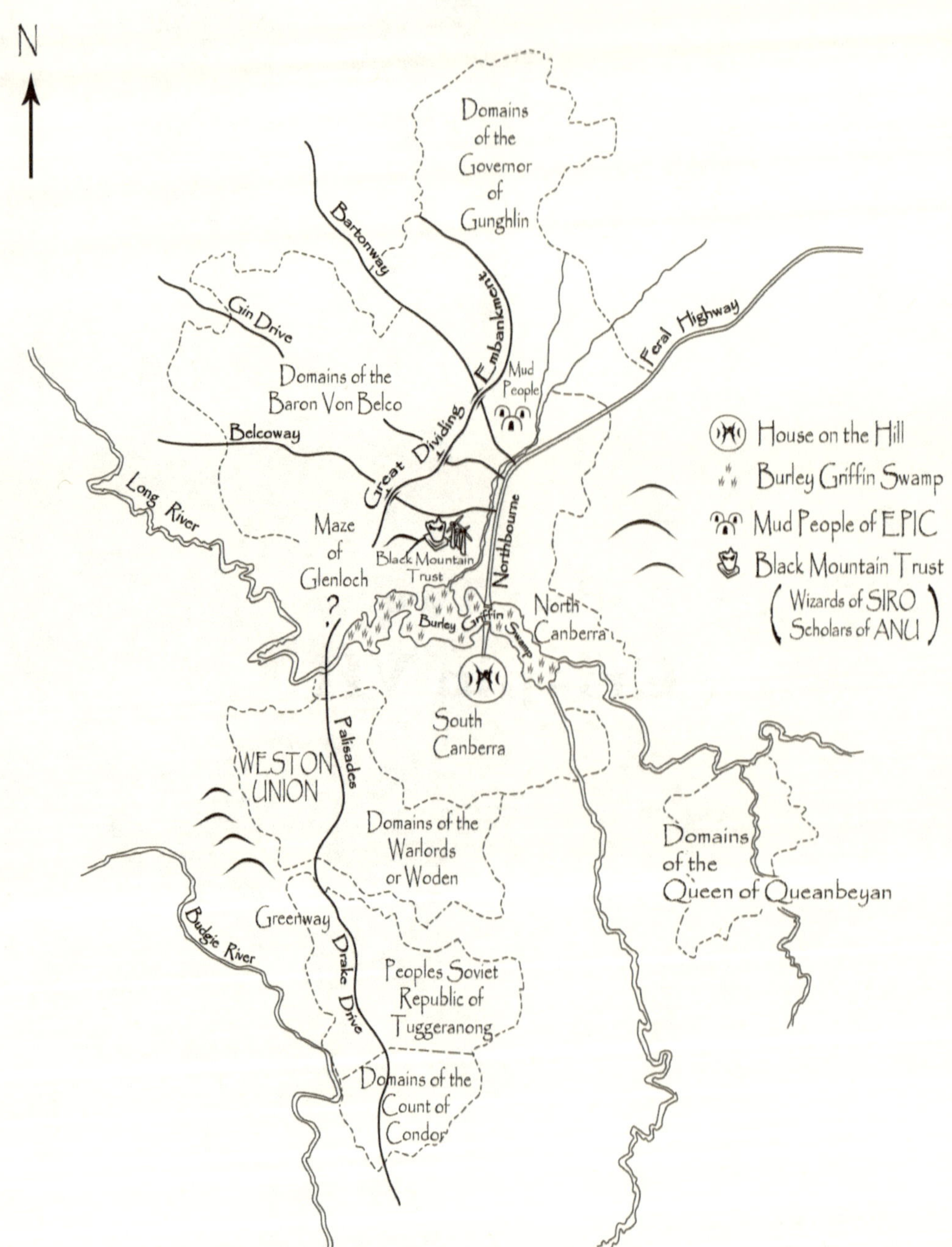

Crispin Spalding would pass into history, as would the civilisation that he had tried so valiantly to defend. He and the other 'ancient ones' of the time before Gaia's Curse would become the stuff of legends.

Six generations would also pass. While the temperature and the CO_2 levels did not climb much higher, neither would they decline for a long time. The people of Canberra would learn to endure heat and drought and dust, and how to trap all the water they could from the occasional heavy downpour. Housing and irrigation systems would become concentrated around the water courses – the Ponds in Gungahlin, Lake Gin in Belco, the Ainslie/O'Connor wetlands in North Canberra, the swamps of Burley Griffin, Lake Tuggeranong and the Queanbeyan and 'Budgie rivers.

Populations would fall by about 20% in each generation, and their resource base even faster. They became technological eunuchs. They had the 'tech-knowledgey' of how all manner of wondrous things were made, but lacked the wherewithal to actually produce them. Theirs became an ad hoc, makeshift, ramshackle technology.

People lived in communities, which became their world. The community members grew their own food in urban cooperatives, fashioned home-made solar panels and windmills to generate just enough electrical power for cooking and some lighting, and cobbled together appliances and equipment from bits and pieces. Their inventions did not work well, but they did work. One scientist, or Wizard as they became known, had described their technology as 'very Heath Robinson'.

Children still learnt the rudiments of reading and writing and 'rithmetic, but that was about as far as most people's education went. In a mainly agricultural society, they could get by without the three Rs. In any case, computers had long since ceased functioning, print was fading in many of the books and paper was in short supply. People clung to vestiges of literacy because they felt it was one of the important legacies of civilisation.

The flame of knowledge was kept burning, on low power, by the Scholars of Anu and the Wizards of SIRO. They acquired almost mystical status in the minds of an ignorant populace.

Yet it was their acolytes who kept the schools running, often in their spare time. They kept their eyes out for bright students, whom they would encourage to continue their education. A chosen few would go on to become Scholars and Wizards, thus perpetuating their special species.

Beyond that, they bided their time. Someday, Gaia's Curse would be lifted, and things would improve. Then, their collective wisdom and 'tech-knowledgey' would become important, as civilisation started to rebuild itself.

3. The President's Dilemma

President Crispin VII stepped outside of the House on the Hill to survey his domain. He was 'master of all he surveys', which was literally true. All of the land to the bare, brown Brindabellas was his realm. Yet it was only a few hundred square kilometres.

In the days of Crispin I, an entire continent of eight million square kilometres had been ruled from this place. That was long, long ago when his palace had been a magnificent edifice, arcing its way across the hill and dominating the South Canberra skyline. Atop it was once a huge triangular steel flagpole, now bent and twisted and rusting away. Many of the rooms in the palace had also crumbled over the centuries. Only the impressive façade, blasted with dust and yellowed with age, and a few rooms at the core of the building remained intact.

Seven generations of Crispin Spaldings had managed to keep the city state of Canberra together, but they'd had to make compromises. They had handed most of their power over to local communities.

The leaders of many communities had grandiose names. Originally, it was all in fun, but over the generations, some of those leaders had started to take their titles seriously as they consolidated smaller communities into larger ones. That was why the Warlord of Woden and the Baron von Belco were now so powerful. Almost too powerful.

Reports had come in that the Baron's troops were massing on the western side of the crumbling remains of the GDE. People had long since forgotten what the GDE stood for, but it was generally taken to mean the Great Dividing Embankment.

The troops assembling there were those of the Caliph of Kaleen and his neighbour, the Grandee of Giralang. They were probably unwilling allies of the Baron, who also had the support of the MacGregor of MacGregor and troops from the Fiefdom of Fraser. The Archon of Aranda seemed to be equivocating.

On the other side of the ridgeline, troops loyal to the Dowager Duchess of Downer, the Wazir of Watson and the Grand Duke of North Lyneham were being mustered. They would need allies, especially if the Governor of Gungahlin and the Mud People of EPIC decided to support the Baron.

The President did think of sending an envoy, the Archbishop of Ainslie, to negotiate a peace settlement, but the Baron von Belco had little time for priests. Already, the Prelate of Page had been driven from his post.

Crispin still had South Canberra under his control: the King of Kingston and the Nabob of Narrabundah were his allies. Would they be able to help? And would he have to work his way through the treacherous algal ponds of Burley Griffin to North Canberra to see for himself what was going on? He looked up at the stub that was all that remained of the once proud Black Mountain Tower. How on earth had the Ancients constructed it? Rumour had it that the tower once contained a revolving restaurant, but his engineers dismissed that idea as fanciful.

So he looked the other way, to the imposing Woden Tower in the south. Would the Warlord be friend or foe?

***

For his part, the Warlord of Woden had problems of his own. He could rely on his deputies, the Pharaoh of Phillip, the Prefect of Pearce and the Sheriff of Stirling, but the Webmaster of Weston and the Chairman of Chapman had already suggested that Weston Creek should secede from the Woden Union.

Further south, the situation was even worse. True, the Tuggeranong Soviet had been successful. The necessity of forming a collective community enterprise was consistent with its Marxist-Leninist ideology. But ideologues are prone to bickering, and the Soviet became rent by factional infighting.

The perfidious Count of Condor had seized his chance. Descendant of a dubious French aristocrat, he believed that the feudal system was the natural order of things. He persuaded the leaders of four neighbouring suburbs to break away with him and create their own domain.

Being reduced to the status of serfs did not appeal to many of his subjects. Some defected to the Tuggeranong Soviet, forcing the Count to erect a fence along Johnson and Woodcock Streets to stop more from fleeing. Then, to cap it off, he had to fend off attacks from the chicken rustlers of the Cooma Confederacy.

The one piece of encouraging news for the Warlord of Woden was that a ginger group had seized power in the Tuggeranong Soviet. Inspired by Lenin and the Bolsheviks, Helen Hart and the Greenway Group had taken control of the Politburo, and were starting to impose order on the fractious Soviet.

***

That was how matters stood in the north, west and south. Meanwhile, in the east, unbeknownst to President Crispin, things were about to become less stable. Doris, the Queen of Queanbeyan was a dear old soul and everybody loved her – everybody, this is, except Jezebel, the Begum of Jerra. She was reputed to be the fairest in the land, even though her skin was of olive complexion. She affected a slight foreign accent to accentuate that she was exotic and mysterious.

Jezebel loved nothing better than to have fawning suitors slobbering at her feet. And she realised she needed an ally if she was to overthrow Queen Doris. She fixed her eyes on Quentin, the youthful new Karabar Khan. He was brave, handsome and stupid. Just the man she wanted.

***

The Baron von Belco looked towards the Black Mountain Tower. The stub was an eyesore. He would like to go up there and pull it down with his bare hands. He was a big, bad Beastly Boy with a bullet shaped head and a bristling ginger moustache.

The Baron was reputed to be the most foul-tempered person in Canberra, a reputation that he did nothing to discourage. He used to walk loudly while carrying a big stick, and he enjoyed nothing more than to give people a damn good thrashing.

He wanted more land, and more peasants to work his land. Like the Count of Condor, he believed that what Canberra needed was the reintroduction of the feudal system. It was the next logical step. None of your mimsy-wimsy namby-pamby democracy for him. The strong had a right to rule, and soon, he would be the strongest of them all.

***

While the President and the Baron were looking towards Black Mountain, a powerful man and an influential woman were meeting just below the mountain itself. They were the principle guardians of the Black Mountain Trust, founded by President Crispin I. By tradition, the Grand Wizard of Siro was named Norman and the High Priestess of Anu was named Maya. They were cousins – descendants of Crispin and Maya Spalding and Norman and Jasmine Tweed.

They were sitting on a terrace outside one of the Siro buildings. Nearby, their disciples were working in the fields: the engineers and electricians were putting together trellises; the chemists were squashing vegetables to make oil which they hoped to turn into battery acid; the botanists were drying papyrus, the poets and historians were, naturally, fermenting some grapes; while the economists were mucking about in the fish ponds.

Above them, they could hear the distant whirr of the windmills on the mountain. To Maya, it was a sound both ominous and mesmerising, yet she knew the windmills generated the electricity that Siro and Anu enjoyed. Even so, she thought of them as the 'mills of the gods'.

Maya handed Norman a set of figures. 'We appear to be approaching equilibrium.'

'In what way?'

'Our demographers reckon that fertility rates are increasing to replacement level. At that rate, our population should stabilise around the hundred thousand mark.'

Norman nodded. 'I guess, given the level of our technology, the amount of water and the quality of soils on the limestone plains, that's about how many people we can support.'

'It used to be over half a million,' she reminded him.

'Yes. When we were the nation's capital and could bring in produce from outside.' There was a sound on his walkie-talkie. 'Excuse me.'

In days of yore, it had been possible to communicate with other centres of learning around the world – islands of wisdom amidst the tides of barbarism. Now, the only means of broadcast communication was by radio, using low power transmissions to those who had crystal sets, and by a few SIRO walkie-talkies.

'Anything of interest?' asked Maya.

Norman nodded. 'My ornithologists report seeing signs of troop movements on the other side of the GDE, in the vicinity of Belcoway.'

'Is the Baron planning to attack North Canberra?'

'Perhaps. Although, I thought his first moves would be against the Gungahlinites, or the Mud People of EPIC. He might not be strong enough to take on Gungahlin, but the Mud People should be an easy target.'

'I don't know about that. They won the Spud Wars with Watson, remember?'

'More's the pity.'

'Why?'

'Because, if they'd lost, they would have been forced to become part of North Canberra,' Norman explained. 'Then, they would have interbred, which would have done wonders for their gene pool.'

'Really?' replied Maya sarcastically. 'Then perhaps it would be good if the Baron's troops invaded North Canberra, ravished the women, and mixed up the gene pool even more.'

Norman shook his head. 'It would not be good news for us. The Baron is contemptuous of the Wizards of Siro, possibly because we're a threat to him. As for culture and learning, his own art form seems to be beating people with his stick.'

Maya nodded. 'And no doubt, he would take over our lands, and force our disciples to work for him. He might keep some of your wizards, but my poets and historians and economists would be forced to work all of the time in the fields, instead of having some allocated for study and composition.'

Norman nodded. 'That is why the Baron must be stopped.'

'At least he hasn't started yet,' said Maya philosophically. 'But I suspect it is just a question of time before he does.'

4. The Flight of the Improbable

In days of yore, the President of Australia travelled in a limousine, escorted by security police on motorbikes. President Crispin VII was transported in a surrey. Its tyres were made of an amalgam of leather, tree sap and eucalyptus oil, and were the closest thing to vulcanised rubber that the Canberrans could devise. They didn't provide much cushion from the bumps and stones in the dirt tracks, but at least, unlike the bicycle tyres of old, they didn't puncture.

The Presidential horse was a surly, mean-looking critter that didn't know when it was well-off. There weren't many horses in Canberra, because of the shortage of fodder. But the horses that did live there were worked pretty hard, being yoked to a plough or having to transport cartloads of produce to the markets. By contrast, the President's horse was only deployed on special occasions, when Crispin VII made one of his few 'state visits' to the districts of his domain.

He was accompanied, on bicycles also with amalgam tyres, by both members of the Presidential Guard, and by the Secretary of the Department. There was only one department, so it didn't need a name. The whole of the Australian Public Service now fitted into one room at Parliament House.

Crispin and his entourage hated working their way through the treacherous swamps and algal blooms of Burley Griffin, but it was the most expeditious way to reach the north. The mighty bridges that had once spanned the lake had long since fallen down.

I should build a bridge across here, he thought. *If we can capture some of the Baron's Beastly Boys, we can use them to make it.*

***

Meanwhile, up at the GDE, the Baron was reviewing his Beastly Boys. He was walking up and down with his stick, while occasionally giving someone a whack. He loved the satisfying smack of stick on snout, or crack on back, or thump on rump. The Baron's men cringed in terror, either from the stick or from his sister, who was walking with him, and snorting like a hippopotamus at anyone doubled up in pain.

When the Baron reached the collapsed remains of Ellen Bridge, he was livid. On either side of the embankment that was once the GDE, the Caliph's and Grand Duke's men had put aside their sticks and were calling out to each other in friendly fashion. Clearly, both sides were hoping this little *contretemps* would soon be over.

'Caliph,' roared the Baron, his ginger moustache bristling, 'get your men into formation. Then go over the top and disembowel the enemy.'

'Effendi,' protested the Caliph. 'The wall is too high. We cannot see how the enemy are deployed.'

The Baron twitched. 'Then bloody well send someone to the top to find out,' he roared.

'The rubble is too dangerous to climb, effendi.'

'Idiot.' The Baron whacked him on the head with his stick. His sister snorted and guffawed. The Baron seethed, and shouted. 'Does anybody have any ideas about how we can see the rabble on the other side of that rubble?'

His Beastly Boys, who weren't noted for their intellectual abilities, probably didn't even know what an idea was. Then a short man with oriental features spoke up. 'In ancient China, they would have sent a man up in a kite, to spy on enemies on the other side.'

The Baron beamed. 'That's a brilliant idea. What is your name?'

'Dinh.'

'Dinh What?'

'My name is Dinh Ling,' said the man, sadly.

The Baron and his men laughed. Dinh hung his head in embarrassment. 'I tell you what, Master Dingaling. You go and build your kite and fly over that embankment and find out what the enemy are up to. When you get back, you can have the hand of my sister Elizabeth in marriage.'

Dinh blanched. Elizabeth leered at him, and licked her lips in a predatory way.

'I – I would be no good. I get vertigo,' protested the little man.

'Well,' said the Baron, 'let me put it to you another way. If you don't go up, I *will* give you in marriage to my sister Elizabeth.'

'I'm going, I'm going.' So Dinh decided to go up, realising that there was no fate worse than Beth.

He went away to build his kite. Later, on the eastern side of the embankment, in a field in North Lyneham, the Grand Duke was sipping tea with the Dowager Duchess of Downer. They could hear the Baron bellowing in the distance.

'The natives are restless tonight,' quipped the Grand Duke.

'I'm sure the poor man has digestive problems. They would account for his disagreeable nature.'

'Perhaps you should send him one of your herbal remedies, Melba dearest.'

'Perhaps I should. Some eucalyptus tea, perhaps.'

'With any luck it might poison him.'

'Now, now, Cossie darling.' She patted him affectionately on his Grand Ducal knee. 'Hist. Listen.'

The Grand Duke keened his ears. In the distance, he could hear the chanting of monks.

'Oh, that's from the monastery in Archie Street. It's Buddha's birthday, or something. Lyneham is prone to sporadic outbreaks of Buddhism.'

'No.' She pointed in the direction of Ellen Street. 'It's a procession.'

'Good Lord. It's the President.'

***

Back on the western side, Dinh Ling was fashioning his kite. In ancient China, it would have been a magnificent silk contrivance with ornate designs of fearsome fire-breathing dragons to scare the enemy. But in the resource-starved world of the 23rd century, he had to make do with an impromptu assortment of bamboo poles, and strips of leather and bark, held together by eucalyptus gum. It didn't look very airworthy, but at least it was aromatic. He wanted a good rope for the tether, but all he could get were old bits knotted together.

A wind had sprung up, quartering between north and west. He tried running into it to get lift, but he fell flat on his face, to the amusement of the aforementioned Beastly Boys. 'The wind isn't strong enough,' he complained to the Baron.

'Then you need something stronger.' The Baron looked around for a tall tree.

At that point, who should turn up but the Grandee of Giralang. He had adopted the speech of an English lord, either to appear to be ineffective and harmless, or to mask the fact that he was. 'Now, I'm given my chaps a jolly good talking to, so they're raring to have a crack at the enemy.'

'Not until we find out where the enemy are,' replied the Baron. 'Which means we have to get Dingaling to go up.'

'Or else, he marries me.' Elizabeth snorted.

'I say, in ancient China, didn't they use hot air balloons or something?'

'We haven't got a hot air balloon,' replied the Baron. 'But you've given me an idea.'

***

Back on the eastern side, the President and his entourage arrived at the tea party.

'Crispin, darling.' The Dowager Duchess gave him a hug. 'Do sit down and have some blackberry tea.'

President Crispin VII lowered himself in a chair, and sipped some tea. It was welcome relief after the tiresome journey. 'Now, what's been happening?'

The Grand Duke peered to the west, where he could see smoke rising. 'Looks like the Baron is lighting a fire, sire.'

***

'The idea is very simple, Dingaling,' explained the Baron as his Beastly Boys raked a batch of glowing coals. 'You run at full speed until you reach the coal patch. Then the hot air will give you the lift you need.'

Dinh cringed. Then he saw Beth's toothy, slobbering grin. He gave a great cry and ran towards the burning coals. He didn't get lift immediately; the hot coals singed his feet. He screamed, and leapt high into the air. Higher and higher he rose, as the wind picked up his kite. The tether of knotted ropes strained to hold on to the kite.

But not for long.

***

'Good lord, what on Earth is that?' The Grand Duke pointed towards the strange contrivance that reared up over the embankment.

'It must be the Baron's secret weapon,' said the President. 'What fiendish cunning.'

'The kite man is babbling in a strange tongue,' remarked the Duchess. 'Is it a war cry?'

The Grand Duke shook his head. 'It might be Chinese, or something. I can't make out what he is saying.'

Dinh didn't know what he was saying either. His brain cells were too preoccupied with his predicament to sort out his garbled vocalisations.

His kite had barely lifted above the crumbled remains of Ellen Bridge, when a sudden wind shift took it further south to where the GDE dipped into a low-lying area between North Lyneham and Kaleen, known as the Valley of Death. There were lookouts posted in the woods on opposite sides, so no-one could attempt to launch an attack across the valley.

The wind shifted back to the west. Dinh drifted along Gin Drive, catching a glimpse of the ruins of the colosseum that had been Canberra's main stadium. Ahead of him, he could see a pagoda. The sounds of chanting grew louder as he approached, until he could see that they were emanating from monks practicing martial arts in the grounds of a temple.

His kite had stayed together remarkably well, in defiance of the laws of structural engineering and aerodynamics. The aroma of eucalyptus was becoming stronger. Heat from the coals melted the gum, and caused it to run. Bits of bark and leather peeled off from his kite.

He screamed as it plunged headlong towards the planet. Fortunately, as its point speared into the ground, the force of impact was dissipated in shattering the kite into dozens of pieces.

While the monks stopped and stared in astonishment, the Lama of Lyneham calmly detached himself from his acolytes and went over to the crumpled mess, in front of a statue.

Dinh was groaning. He had concussion and fractured ribs. Every limb and muscle in his body was bruised and strained.

'All things are an illusion, my son,' the Lama told him. 'Even your pain is an illusion.'

In his dazed state, Dinh looked up, not at the Lama but at the statue from which he thought the voice had come. The benign face of the Buddha beamed down at him.

Thus it was that Dinh Ling became a convert.

5. Embankment

Having satisfied himself that the communities of North Canberra had enough cohesion to keep their district intact, President Crispin VII returned to Parliament House. On the other hand, Baron von Belco was furious that his plans had been thwarted. His ginger moustache bristled. 'Why am I surrounded by idiots?'

The Caliph of Kaleen and the Grandee of Giralang exchanged an awkward look.

'Effendi,' said the Caliph. 'You said you only wanted stupid people to serve you. In case someone got ideas above their station.'

The Baron nodded, wryly. He looked out at his Beastly Boys, a motley assortment of misfits who were marching up and down chanting:

With hobnail boots, we trample on our foes
With hobnail boots, we stomp on all their toes.

The minstrel who had penned those lines hadn't been smart enough to think of any more, which didn't really matter because the troops would have been incapable of remembering them anyway.

'Hmm.' The Baron growled. The crumbling remains of the GDE were proving an effective barrier to his attempts to capture North Canberra. He could consider marching north and invading from east of the GDE, but that meant dealing with the Governor of Gungahlin and the Mud People of EPIC.

Instead, he looked towards Black Mountain. The stub of the tower was still an eyesore that he would like to remove.

'I say,' suggested the Grandee, 'couldn't we install a lookout up there?'

'With you on top of it,' taunted the Baron.

'No,' replied the Grandee. 'But I could send up some of my minions.'

What good would that do?' asked the Caliph.

'Well, when they saw the coast was clear—'

'We can't see the coast from here,' retorted the Caliph. 'Not yet, anyway.'

'When they saw that the coast was clear,' insisted the Grandee, 'we could invade.'

'Invade what?' asked the Baron.

'The next place on from Black Mountain is Siro. Oh.' The Grandee was crestfallen. He added in hushed tones. 'Isn't that where the you-know-whats are?'

'What?'

'They who must not be named,' the Grandee said as loudly as he dared.

'The Wizards of Siro?' asked the Baron, scornfully.

'Please, Baron. We dare not utter that name aloud.'

'I just did.' Facing Black Mountain, the Baron roared, 'the Wizards of Siro are a pack of useless wankers.'

The Grandee and the Caliph cringed. They expected a thunderbolt to come forking out of a clear, blue sky. The Baron blew a raspberry at the mountain. Silence. You could have heard a pin drop, but nobody happened to be carrying one.

'You see. Nothing happened.' The Baron laughed. 'Let us go and see the Archon of Aranda. He might know a way across the mountain.'

***

The Archon of Aranda was a wily old man with a bald pate and a long beard. 'Across the mountain, you say? Ooh. Tricky.'

'But can it be done?' demanded the Baron.

'Hmm. Very tricky. Ever tried getting through the Maze of Glenloch? Most places, there is only one embankment, but at Glenloch there are many. You could wander around in there for days. And if you did get through, you might find yourself in the swamps of Burley Griffin.'

'There are monsters in those swamps,' wailed the Caliph.

'Monsters, Wizards.' The Baron snorted. 'Any other bright ideas?'

'Well,' suggested the Archon, 'you could always try dismantling the GDE at the eastern end of Belcoway.'

'What good would that do?'

'I have an old map which shows that, once upon a time, Belcoway extended right through to Civic. If you could break through there, you could march all the way into the heart of North Canberra.'

'Really?' The Baron's eyes lit up, which was frightening.

'But effendi, it would be very dangerous,' warned the Caliph. 'The Oligarch of O'Connor and the Tyrant of Turner would attack you from the left and the Wizards of Siro and the Scholars of Anu would attack you from the right.'

'You said *you*.' The Baron glared, menacingly. '*You* would be attacked. If we go through, we all go through.' He added mockingly. 'Including you, effendi.'

'Oh.' The Grandee felt rather faint. He mopped his brow.

'What's the matter with you?'

'Well, don't you think…What I mean is…Perhaps the GDE is meant to be there.'

'Of course it's meant to be there,' retorted the Baron. 'Somebody built it.'

'Maybe it was meant to be a barrier. You know, keep the barbarians outside the Great Wall, and all that sort of thing.'

'Maybe,' suggested the Archon, 'it was built to protect Belco from the tribes of North Canberra. A barrier works both ways, you know.'

The Baron paced up and down, wielding his stick. He whacked it against the trunk of a sapling, which snapped in two. 'Grandee, Caliph, Archon. Gather your troops. We march against the embankment at Belcoway tomorrow. If we can't get over the top of it, then we'll pull it to pieces with our bare hands, and force our way through.'

The Grandee looked ruefully at his palms. He did not have the hands of a bear. Seeing the Baron stride off into the distance, he turned to face his companions. 'He really has gone too far this time, you know.'

'Agreed,' said the Caliph. 'But you know what would happen if we refused to obey him.'

The Grandee winced as he remembered the last beating he'd had from the beastly Baron, and the one before that, and the one before that. He trembled. 'There must be something we can do. Could we attack and yet not attack, if you know what I mean.'

'No,' replied the Caliph.

'I think I do,' said the Archon. 'We must ensure that our troops are incompetent invaders.'

'That wouldn't be difficult,' retorted the Caliph. 'But leave it to me. I think I can ensure that the Baron's plans will be thwarted.'

***

Towards sunset that day, Captain Guard was patrolling the crumbling remains of the GDE near Ellen Bridge. His name was Trex Guard and he was Captain of the Guard, so it worked out neatly.

He heard a whoosh, and looked up to see an arrow flying over the wall. He smiled. He knew what that meant.

The Grand Duke of North Lyneham was sipping tea with

his friend, confidant, and probable paramour the Dowager Duchess of Downer when Captain Guard approached him. 'Message from the Caliph, sir.'

The Grand Duke removed a scroll of papyrus that had been wrapped around the arrow and read it – the papyrus that is, not the arrow.

'Hmm. This is serious.'

'What is it, Cossie darling?' asked the Duchess.

'Another one of the Baron's nefarious schemes I'm afraid, Melba dear. We shall have to arrange a little surprise for him.'

***

Next morning, a coalition of the largely unwilling assembled near the western side of the ruins of the GDE, where it had collapsed on Belcoway. They were a motley band of fifty or so souls, many of whom looked like they had been pressed into service at the last minute.

The Baron addressed them. 'All right. I don't care if you climb over the wall, tunnel through it or pull it down. Just get to the other side.' He motioned to his lieutenant, Sergeant Percival Owwible.

Sergeant Owwible drew in his breath, puffed out his cheeks and shouted, 'cheearge!'

A bewildered group of troops started moving towards the wall at varying speeds until the Baron held them up. 'Sergeant Owwible.'

'Sah.'

The Baron put a brotherly arm around the sergeant, who looked worried, with good reason. 'This is meant to be a surprise attack.'

'Sah.'

'That means that silence is essential, doesn't it?'

'Yes, Sah. I suppose it does.'

'Then do it quietly,' roared the Baron, and hit him with his rhythm stick.

'Charge,' yelled Sergeant Owwible quietly. It sounded nasal because he was holding a bloodied nose.

The Baron's own Beastly Boys clambered up the wall like the band of supercharged nutniks that they were. They soon came sliding down, bringing odd bits of masonry with them. They looked like the Keystone Cops on a particularly bad day. The other troops approached the wall more tentatively.

'Excuse me, sir,' said Private Underling, who was one of the Grandee's militia. 'The archway at the far left end hasn't collapsed as much as the others. It might be possible to tunnel our way through there.'

'Off you go then,' said the Baron.

Underling disappeared into a pile of rubble. The others heard rumblings for several minutes and then a muffled voice: 'I'm through.'

The Baron ordered his troops to halt, which, since they had to do it quietly, took a while. 'Right. Pull out the rubble there, and we'll have a nice little archway to march through.'

So the troops formed a chain and pulled out bits of rubble. Half an hour later, they had cleared a passageway to the other side. It wasn't very wide and they had to clamber through. The Baron ordered them to clear some more rubble, making a large enough passage for him to proceed in some style.

'At last,' cried the Baron, as he stepped into North Canberra. He looked about him at the Promised Land. Silence had been unnecessary. There wasn't a soul in sight. 'Right,' he said, gleefully. 'Let the invasion begin.'

6. The Battle of Belcoway

Baron von Belco stood hands on hips as he stared: Belcoway snaked off into a wasteland. The Caliph of Kaleen, the Grandee of Giralang and the Archon of Aranda stood beside him.

'Desolate, isn't it?' commented the Archon, hoping to deter the Baron.

'Forward,' shouted the Baron. He strode along the crumbling highway, stick under his arm, looking like a drum major at a parade. His followers shambled along behind him.

Ere long, they came to a fork in the road.

'Where to now, effendi?' asked the Caliph.

'I do have a map,' offered the Archon. 'It's very old, but you can just make out some of the details.' He took out a large, tattered, sheet of paper of many folds that threatened to fall apart even as he opened it up.

The map was so old that many of the street names and other features had long since faded. What remained was sufficient to indicate that Belcoway forked into two parts.

'What are these faint pink lines?' asked the Baron.

'I believe they were once bright red lines.' The Archon traced his finger over them. They mark out the territorial boundaries. The left fork goes straight through O'Connor, while the right passes between Turner and Anu, enroute to Civic.'

'In that case,' said the Baron, 'we'll take the fork to the right. If we can capture Civic, we can use it as a base to attack the rest of North Canberra.'

'I say,' said the Grandee, 'shouldn't we do some reconnaissance?'

'Off you go then.'

The Grandee was aghast. 'Me?'

The Baron put a fatherly arm around the Grandee's shoulder. 'Tell you what. You and your band of misfits take the left fork, while the rest of us go to the right.'

'But that will take us into the heart of enemy territory.'

'Which will divert them while we outflank them. Divide and conquer.'

Conquer who? thought the Grandee.

Minutes later, while the Baron and most of his troops marched to the right, the Grandee and his ungallant band of a dozen headed the other way. It wasn't that they were timid – well, some of them were less endowed with courage than the others – it was just that they didn't really have their hearts in it.

Once the parties had advanced far enough up their respective forks to be out of sight of each other, Lieutenant Shrubsole said quietly to the Grandee, 'it's rather hot, sir, and we are getting tired.' He motioned towards a clump of trees.

The Grandee mopped his fevered brow. 'Yes. Jolly good idea.' It would give him time to think of an excuse why he and his militia didn't manage to penetrate as far into enemy territory as the Baron would have liked – an excuse that meant being only lightly flogged.

As they decamped among the trees, the Grandee keened his ears to listen out for the slightest sign of danger. Apart from a few bird calls, there was silence.

The Grandee motioned to two of his troops to creep ahead and see if the coast was clear. They returned moments later, their heads shaking with disbelief. One of them said quietly, 'I think you'd better come and see this for yourself, sir.'

***

Meanwhile, the tunnelling exploits of the Baron's brigade had not gone unnoticed. High up on Black Mountain, two ornithologists from Siro were doing the bird census when they saw a white cloud in the distance.

'Smoke?' queried Orni #1.

Orni #2 trained his ancient binoculars on it. He shook his head. 'Looks like dust.'

Orni #1 took her turn with the binoculars. 'Good Lord. Something is happening at the GDE on Belcoway.'

They reported their sightings to the Grand Wizard. He sent scouts to spy on the rag-tag band, led by a pompous red headed man with a stick, as they marched towards North Canberra. He reported to the High Priestess of Anu. 'They've split into two groups, but most of them are headed this way.'

'Right.' The High Priestess sent one messenger to notify the Tyrant of Turner, and another to the Chief Musician of Anu.

'Splendid,' said the Chief Musician, with a mad gleam in his eyes. 'We can entertain them with my concerto for vuvuzela, saxophone and didgeridoo, Opus three.'

***

The Grandee of Giralang and his band crept through the trees until they came in sight of a clearing. They stared in amazement. A young man was making bird calls as he walked around with a clipboard.

'Shall we nab him, sir?' asked Lieutenant Shrubsole quietly.

'No. Leave this to me.' The Grandee felt a surge of courage. 'Well, hello there,' he said as he emerged from the foliage. 'Lovely day.'

'It's simply marvellous, isn't it? Who are you?'

'My name is Algernon.'

'Interesting name. I'm Gerald.'

'That's an interesting name, too.' As the two men shook hands, the Grandee wondered where he'd heard it before.

Lieutenant Shrubsole had another quiet word with his fearless leader. 'Isn't he the son of the Oligarch of O'Connor?'

The Grandee stroked his chin beard. 'Could be.'

'In case you're wondering,' Gerald explained, 'I'm doing the bird count.'

'The bird count?'

'Yes. For the Siro bird census.'

The Grandee stared at him with a mixture of reverence and fear. 'Are you a wizard or an acolyte?' His men cringed in terror at the mention of those words.

The young man had a nervous laugh. 'Dear me, no. I'm just a Friend of Siro. There are lots of bird watchers all over Canberra. We help out with the census.'

'What sorts of birds are you finding?'

Mynahs and magpies mostly, but we get the occasional parrot.' He added sadly, 'we used to get water fowl, but our wetlands have mainly dried up.'

A wicked thought came to the Grandee's mind. 'Well, actually, I think I know a place where there might be some water fowl.'

'Really?' The young man's face brightened.

'Yes. I'm afraid it's a little way from here, but perhaps I could show it to you someday … Er, I and my friends are on a nature ramble, and actually, we've got ourselves rather lost. I wonder if you could show us the way back to the fork in the road.'

'Well,' said Gerald doubtfully, 'I don't want to go too far from home, because I have to report to Diana.'

'Diana?'

'My sister. I tell her where the mynah birds are and she hunts them with her bow and arrows. Actually, I think she'd like to shoot men too, but Father is very important and he won't let her. Just as well for you.' He gave a nervous laugh.

Again, the quiet voice of Lieutenant Shrubsole in his master's ear: 'Didn't Diana hunt the ancient Geeks?'

'Ancient Greeks.'

'Greeks, Geeks, what's the difference?'

The Grandee decided that the gap in his lieutenant's education was too great to bridge. 'She used to roam around in the moonlight in her nightie and lure young men to a sacred grove, where she fired arrows at them.'

'That's just like my sister,' chirped up Gerald. 'She could be hunting right now.'

'In her nightie?' The Grandee's troops were now terribly interested in the conversation.

'Not usually.'

***

Meanwhile, the Baron and his ragged band were almost within sight of Civic. The Archon held the fragments of his tattered map as they marched. 'Should be just around the next corner.'

But when they rounded the corner, there was a reception committee waiting for them – the Tyrant of Turner and his troops. Descendants of academics and departmental secretaries, they were a mean looking bunch.

The Tyrant had one hand on his hip, and was leaning casually on a quarter stave. He wore the hooded cloak that was his symbol of office. 'Nice of you to pay us a visit, Baron.'

The Baron did a quick mental calculation. His force outnumbered the Tyrant's by about two to one. 'Bow down before me, Termite of Turner. Your lands are now mine.'

'Is that a fact?' The Tyrant pulled back his hood and lifted his stave. 'Shall we put that to the test? Of course, being the gutless cur that you are, you wouldn't dare take me on.'

His ginger moustache bristling, the Baron advanced. Both men raised their sticks in a salute. Then battle began. The Baron lashed out with blow after blow, but the Tyrant grabbed his stave with both hands and parried them.

The Archon, who was folding his map, was puzzled. The Tyrant was fighting in a purely defensive way. Was he playing for time until reinforcements arrived?

The Baron surprised the Tyrant with a quick jab rather than a downwards blow. It glanced off the Tyrant's shoulder, causing him to wince. He switched to single-handed combat.

Sensing a movement in his peripheral vision, the Caliph tugged the Archon's sleeve, and pointed to the right, where a group of hooded brethren were gathering – the dreaded wizards and scholars of Siro and Anu.

They raised vuvuzelas to their lips and produced an unearthly sound that caused the Baron's troops to quake with fear. 'We are accursed,' cried one.

Even the Baron was distracted. He had drawn his stick out to the right. The Tyrant attacked it with a short sharp blow that sent it flying out of the Baron's hands. Seizing the moment, he cried, 'charge!'

The Baron and his band beat a hasty retreat up the road with the Tyrant and his troops in hot pursuit, and the vuvuzelas wailing in the background. By the time they reached the fork in the road, both sides were tiring. The Tyrant called off the chase, but not before he had given the Baron a whack on the derriere.

'And don't come back,' shouted the Tyrant.

Orni #1 and Orni #2 tracked the retreating rabble to the crumbling remains of the GDE, watching in amusement as the Baron and his band disappeared into the stonework.

7. Kidnapped

The Tyrant of Turner adjusted his hood and led his troops back to Turner. As he raised his arm to give the 'thumbs up' sign to the vuvuzela players from Anu, he winced. The Baron had given him a nasty jab with his stick.

The heroic defenders returned to Turner to the cheers of some of the Tyrant's subjects. An acolyte of the Black Mountain Trust, he was a popular ruler, whose title was more for the purposes of alliteration than to suggest he was an absolute dictator. A few well-meaning citizens patted him on the shoulder, which, under the circumstances, was not something he appreciated. Retreating to his modest apartment, he removed his hooded cloak with difficulty.

'Have a nice war today, dear?' asked Mrs Tyrant as she helped him remove his shirt.

'Thanks to me and my gallant band, you have been saved from being ravished by the Baron and his brutes.'

'Lucky old me … Ooh. That will swell up something nasty. We'll have to get some ointment from the herbalist for that.'

In an age when doctors were in short supply, the local herbalist-cum-midwife was an important member of the community. Deirdre was a middle-aged woman who supplemented her income with love potions and fortune telling.

'Dearie, that's a terrible bruise you've got there,' she said as she ran her hands gently over the Tyrant's shoulder. 'We'll have to put a poultice on that one. And some padding for your other shoulder as well.'

'But my left shoulder is fine.'

'Yes, but your right one is so swelled up that with the poultice on top, you're going to look as lop sided as a hunchback.'

'Like Richard the Third?'

'Third what?'

'Now is the winter of our discontent made glorious by the summer sun of York,' he declaimed.

'If you say so, dearie. York? Is that somewhere near Wagga?' As she applied the poultice, she asked, 'Now, is there anything else you'd like? Your fortune told, maybe?'

'No, thank you. I believe we are masters of our own destinies.'

'Oh, I wouldn't be too sure of that. Just look what happened to Gerald.'

'The son of the Oligarch of O'Connor?'

'That's him. Kidnapped he was.'

The Tyrant was surprised. 'When?'

'While you were thumping the Baron. The Grandee of Giralang spirited him away through a tunnel. The orniwhatsits found his clipboard.'

'Where?'

'By the GDE.'

'Oh, great.' The Tyrant slumped back into a chair, and winced. 'That's all we need.'

***

The circumstances of Gerald's abduction had been as much a matter of chance as they were of calculation.

'I must admit I'm not an expert on water fowl,' confessed the Grandee as they had walked along. 'We used to get a duck with a black streak over its eye.'

'The black duck, *Anas superciliosa*,' Gerald informed him.

'If you say so. I haven't seen many about lately. I'm not sure what happened to them.'

'They were delicious,' said Lieutenant Shrubsole.

The Grandee glared at him, then spoke quietly. 'I can't be entirely sure, but the other night, I thought I saw a black swan.'

'Really?' Gerald's eyes looked like they were going to pop out of his head. 'I thought they were extinct.'

'We do have some seagulls,' added Private Underling.

'Silver gulls,' Gerald corrected him.

As they walked and talked, the Grandee realised that he had a dilemma. He genuinely liked Gerald, who was one of the few people he had met with whom he could have an intelligent conversation, even if it was limited to ornithological matters. But he realised that if he was to appease the Baron, he would have to take Gerald prisoner. For his part, Gerald felt a strange attraction for this elegant stranger.

They were so engrossed in their conversation, that they scarcely noticed they had walked all the way to the tunnel that the Baron's troops had fashioned at the remains of the GDE. Gerald was alarmed. 'Are you from the other side?'

'Us? We, er, we are the Belco Ramblers, aren't we lads?' They grunted in agreement. 'Anyway, we found this nice little tunnel in the wall. And we'd always wanted to see North Canberra, so we thought, I don't think anyone would mind if we went for a little ramble.'

'Well, it's been nice meeting all of you,' said Gerald, 'but I really think I should be going back home.

Distracted, the Grandee was staring up the road. 'I'm afraid it might be a little late for that.' He pointed to a ragged band of misfits approaching them, led by an exasperated ginger-haired man who was stickless and rubbing his derriere.

'It's the Baron.'

'Oh, lord.' Startled, Gerald dropped his clipboard. Or perhaps he did it on purpose.

'Quick, through here,' urged the Grandee. Gerald had little choice but to follow him. When they got to the other side, the Grandee added, 'Listen: whatever I say, just go along with it. I may be able to keep you out of his clutches.'

Ere long, the Baron had hobbled his way through the tunnel, to find the Grandee standing there, grinning.

'What are you smirking about?' demanded the Baron.

'Baron, I'd like you to meet my new friend, Gerald.' The Baron gave him a blank look. 'Son of the Oligarch of O'Connor. He's come to see some of our wildlife.'

'Wildlife, eh?' The Baron grinned, wickedly. 'Some of the life in my domain is wild. Very wild.' His brain began ticking over as fast as it could, which would probably have given a snail a run for its money.

Gerald stood there, dumbfounded. He was feeling more uncomfortable by the moment.

'Come along, Gerald,' the Grandee assured him as he put an arm on his shoulder. 'It's not far to our wetlands.'

***

The Baron allowed Gerald to go with the Grandee. He returned home, where news of his disaster had preceded him. Bad news really does travel fast.

His gruesome sister Beth stood on the doorstep of what passed for their baronial mansion. Based on the shell of an ancient government three-bedroom house, it was more impressive than the ramshackle huts in which most of his subjects lived.

'So, beaten off by an old hoodie with a stick and some silly horn players.' She snortled, which was a cross between a snort and a chuckle.

'That old hoodie still packs a mean punch. Besides, it was only a reconnaissance mission. We gathered valuable intelligence.'

'Intelligence, brother dear?' She snortled again. 'Well don't strain your brain too hard trying to work out what it means.'

'It means we'll be better prepared next time.' The Baron looked around for a new stick to beat people with.

'So will they,' she retorted.

There were times when the Baron had to admit that his sister was smarter than she looked, which would not have been difficult.

'And we took a prisoner,' he added.

'Big deal.'

'Yes. No less than the son of the Oligarch of O'Connor. He might be a gormless pretty boy, but we can use him to bargain—'

'Did you say pretty?' There was a lustful look in her eyes.

'I suppose you could call him pretty,' the Baron conceded. 'He's a bird watcher who is about as useless as you. The two of you would make ...' He trailed off. A wicked idea was forming in his mind.

***

When the Oligarch of O'Connor heard that Gerald had been kidnapped by the beastly Baron and his fiends, he had mixed feelings. Gerald, with his ornithological obsessions, was an embarrassment, but it would not reassure his subjects that their fearless leader had failed to prevent the abduction of his own son. What he feared most was that the Baron now had some hold on him. What sort of ransom would he demand for the safe return of Gerald?

Next day, he received a message from the other side of the GDE:

Dear Oligarch of O'Connor,

Your son Gerald is my prisoner. If you do not offer to negotiate for his release in the next three days, I shall marry him to my sister Beth.

Baron von Belco.

At first, the Oligarch was tempted to reply that the Baron could keep Gerald. But then the nasty thought: if Gerald was forcibly married to the Baron's sister, that would make her his daughter-in-law. He blanched. He had seen the Baron's sister and was appalled.

'Woe is me,' he said theatrically, as he put his hand to his head.

'What's the matter, father?'

The Oligarch looked up. Diana, his daughter, was tall and willowy, and dressed in a greenish-grey outfit. She was carrying her bow and a quiver of arrows. He showed her the note.

'Oh, goodie. Does that mean I can have Gerald's room? It's bigger than mine.'

'I thought you'd show a bit more concern for your brother than that.'

'Well, if you think I'm going to rescue him, you've got another think coming.'

'You have another think. If Gerald marries her, Beth von Belco would become your sister-in-law.'

'Oh, yuk! I suppose I'd better rescue him, then.'

'In that case, you'd better start with the Grandee of Giralang. He's rumoured to be looking after Gerald. He's a nice man. Don't be cruel to him.'

***

Gerald had to admit that being a prisoner of the Grandee of Giralang was not so bad. There weren't many water fowl – the marshes near the Grandee's home having largely dried up, but the Grandee was ever so kind to him, and there were some wild flowers to look at, which both men appreciated. It was the start of a beautiful friendship.

Next day, a sedan chair carried by four sweating flunkies turned up on the Grandee's door step. The Baron alighted, with his sister in tow. The Grandee and Gerald blanched at the sight of them.

Beth leered at Gerald, and slobbered. 'He's pretty. I want him.'

The Baron chuckled. 'Unless his father agrees to my ransom terms, he's all yours.'

'Oh, crikey.' Gerald stepped back behind the Grandee.

The Grandee was caught in a terrible bind. While he may have found his soul mate, he didn't fancy tangling with the beastly Baron and his ghastly sister. 'Er, let's not get too hasty.

The Oligarch still has two days in which to agree to your terms.'

The Baron grinned, wickedly. 'You don't think he's going to agree, do you? Not since it means his men will have to clear away the rubble on Belcoway.'

'So you can attack North Canberra whenever you like?'

'So *we* can attack whenever we like. You're in this with me, Grandee.' The Baron chuckled. 'Perhaps we can capture Gerald's sister, and marry her off to someone.' He looked directly at the Grandee.

'You'll never capture my sister,' said Gerald defiantly. 'She's more than a match for your troops, Baron.'

'Which is why I want her on my side.' The Baron ushered his sister into their sedan. 'Gee up.' His weary flunkeys lifted it up. 'Two days, Gerald, and your lonely bachelor nights will be over.' As the sedan departed, the Baron hummed the wedding march.

Gerald bit his finger nails. 'What are we going to do?'

'Fear not.' The Grandee smiled, reassuringly. 'I shall devise a cunning plan.'

8. Rescue

All her cunning and stealth were not enough for Diana to avoid the sharp eyes of Captain Guard, chief security officer of the Grand Duke of North Lyneham. Wearing a hooded cloak, she was creeping along in the shadows of the GDE near Ellen Bridge when he called out to her.

'You are far from your hunting grounds, milady.'

She looked up at him, pulled back her hood and scowled. 'I'm trying to find a way through this stupid wall.'

He wondered why she was trying to break through so far north of O'Connor. Then he remembered that this was the closest the wall got to Giralang.

'Going to rescue Gerald, are we?' he asked, condescendingly.

'No,' she replied, sarcastically, 'We will hunt mynah birds together.'

'Hmm. Can I suggest you try further around, at the Barton Bridge, which collapsed long ago? Also, it means that you will not have to cross through the heartlands of Kaleen.'

'Where is this Barton Bridge?'

'Come. I will show you.'

'I'm quite capable of finding it myself, thank you.'

'I dare say you are capable of many things, mostly bloodthirsty, which is why I insist on escorting you through the Grand Duke's domain.' He pointed to the collapsed remains of the Ellen Bridge. 'I feared that you might try to get through there, but it is heavily guarded by the Caliph's men.'

'They don't scare me.'

'Nor me either. But if you are to succeed, the element of surprise is essential.'

As the two of them walked the kilometre or so through broken ground to the Barton Bridge, he tried to appraise her slender nubile form without obviously leering. She tried to ignore her feelings about the manly self-confidence he exuded as he strolled alongside her.

They reached the crumbled assortment of dirt, concrete blocks and metal strands that were the remains of the Barton Bridge. It had long since compacted into unsightly rubble.

Captain Guard shook his head. 'Hmm. This doesn't look very promising. It may be too dangerous to climb.'

'Nonsense,' retorted Diana and started to clamber up the slope. She came sliding back down amid a shower of concrete, stones and dirt.

The captain caught her as she fell; lowering her gently to the ground, he held on to her a moment or two longer than was necessary. Diana's face was flushed. She hadn't felt this way about a mere man before.

'The GDE does drop away to ground level further along,' he explained. 'But that may be patrolled by the troops of the Governor of Gungahlin.'

'They don't frighten me,' she insisted.

'That is not the point. Our relations with the Governor are cautious. There has been no conflict between us, but he is wary of us and we of him. We don't want an incident to stir up trouble, especially if it drove him into the arms of the Baron von Belco – metaphorically speaking, of course.'

'You talk posh for a guard.'

'I shall take that as a compliment.' They walked along a few hundred metres further to where the embankment had dropped down to an ill-defined track in the waste land. It was all that remained of the once-mighty Gungahlin Drive.

He looked around him. 'Hmm. I can't see any of the Governor's men, but he might have an observation post on yonder hill. You would do well to wait until darkness.'

'If I wait until then,' Diana replied, 'I won't be able to get Gerald back before midnight, which is well past his bed time.'

'I would have thought that was the least of your considerations. However, I can continue my patrol eastwards along our borders; I may be able to distract the guards, if guards there be. Do you know the way?'

Diana unrolled a scroll of papyrus, a product on which the Black Mountain Trust had a monopoly. It was a copy of a map, traced from much older documents. 'I continue up the Bartonway for two kilometres, then make my way across to … Cucumber Street in Giralang.'

He looked at the map. 'You will have to traverse two kilometres of open ground to reach the woodlands of Giralang.'

'If I am detected, I am capable of looking after myself, thank you.'

'To the detriment of whatever poor soul you encountered, no doubt. At least, you haven't brought your bow and arrows with you.'

'Of course not. They would be too conspicuous. But I have this.' She whipped out a large, sharp hunting knife.

Shaking his head, Captain Guard scanned the horizon for signs of the Gungahlin guards. When he looked back, Diana had already vanished.

***

Nimbly working her way past the debris on the north side of the bridge, Diana sprinted along the crumbling remains of Bartonway until she reached the shelter of a grove of trees at the edge of Giralang.

In an age when populations had declined markedly, and it was difficult to transport things over any great distance, most of the suburbs had been turned into farmlands or vegetable gardens. Thus was it so at Giralang.

Diana waited in the trees for the sun to go down. There were sheep grazing in the paddocks, and she was tempted to take a pot shot at them, until she realised that didn't have her bow and arrows. She felt naked without them. Thoughts of nakedness caused her unaccountably to think of Captain Guard.

When the shadows lengthened, she made her way silently from grove to grove, always looking out in case she was seen. Twice, she had to duck back under cover when barking dogs caused their owners to come out and investigate.

On reaching the broad, curling track of Cucumber Street, she headed southwards in the twilight. She walked casually along the road, because, having penetrated so far into enemy territory, people would not be suspicious of her if she acted normally. But when she heard voices a little way behind her, she instinctively ducked for cover behind some bushes.

Two people walked past her, in animated conversation. They said something about 'going to a wedding'.

Her ears pricked up. Was Gerald being married off to the Baron's sister already? Could Diana get there in time to prevent the ceremony?

Following on discretely behind the couple, she soon saw lights in the distance. As she got closer, she could see a gathering of many people in an open area. Ducking behind some more bushes, she crept silently closer.

***

The Prelate of Page generally didn't do weddings, but times were tough, especially since he was at odds with the Baron, who was a virulent atheist. 'Is there any reason,' he intoned, 'why this couple should not be joined in holy matrimony?'

'Yes,' cried out a voice from the back of the assembled crowd. A young woman, clad in green and brown, and holding a large knife, made her way through the startled throng, which quickly parted.

Gerald stood beside the Grandee. Both men were finely attired. Diana pointed her knife at Gerald. 'That man is being forcefully married against his will.'

The Prelate looked at Gerald. 'Is this true?'

'No, I—'

'Of course it's true.' Diana grabbed her brother's arm, and pulled him away from the Grandee. 'Don't worry, darling, I'll get you home safely.'

'But I don't want to go.'

'Go. Of course you want to go. You don't want to marry the Baron's sister, do you?'

'No. But—'

'Then let's go.'

'I'm not marrying her. I want to be with Algernon.'

'Who?'

'The Grandee. We're getting married now.'

Diana was flustered. 'But you can't marry a man.'

'Why not? People marry men all the time.'

'What I mean is, you can't marry another man.'

'Oh, yes he can,' interjected the Grandee. 'Same sex couples are allowed to marry.'

Gerald nodded. 'And if we get married, the Baron can't marry me to his sister.'

'But you can marry the Baron's sister,' suggested the Grandee. 'Or the Baron.'

'Though I'd rather you didn't,' added Gerald. 'I don't want them as in-laws.'

Diana scowled at him. 'I'm not going to marry anyone.' As soon as she said that, the image of Captain Guard came into her mind. She was nonplussed. 'Well, what am I going to tell Father? I'm supposed to rescue you.'

'Well, you can rescue him and abduct me if you like,' suggested the Grandee. 'But please wait until the ceremony is completed.'

***

Captain Guard waited anxiously in the shadows of the Barton Bridge. A trio of goons from the Governor of Gungahlin had arrived and called out to a trio of guards of the Caliph of Kaleen. Soon, they were having a jolly old chinwag, while swigging from a flagon and smoking some funny weeds. Eavesdropping, he learnt of the impending marriage of Gerald and the Grandee.

He wondered how Diana, whether successful in her rescue mission or not, was going to get past the guards. The moon rose. That would make it even harder for her.

He was startled when he heard a female voice, singing. There, standing on a hillock and silhouetted against the moon was a shapely figure who was taking her hooded cloak off.

My, she does look lovely in profile, he thought. The guards thought so too. After pinching themselves to make sure they weren't hallucinating, they made off towards the hill. They were about halfway up when she turned and sprinted down to the roadway.

In the meantime, two figures slunk across the road.

'Good evening, gentlemen,' said Captain Guard quietly, 'and congratulations.'

'Thank you,' replied the Grandee. 'We are in the territory of North Lyneham, I take it.'

'You are indeed.'

'Oh, safe at last,' breathed Gerald.

'In that case,' added the Grandee, 'I wish to claim political asylum, and to seek the protection of the Oligarch of O'Connor.'

'I would escort you thence,' replied Captain Guard as he stared up the road, 'but I suspect I shall be otherwise occupied.'

The two newlyweds followed his gaze. Diana was now sprinting eastwards along the track that was once Gungahlin Drive, with an eager band of guards in pursuit.

'Where is that girl going?' asked the Grandee.

'Drawing off your potential pursuers, I should imagine. Now, I suggest you head down Bartonway and turn right into Ellen Street. From there, you can make your way to Lyneham and thence to O'Connor. It will be a long walk, I'm afraid.'

***

Meanwhile, Diana was having the time of her life, sprinting in the moonlight while being pursued by several men who weren't very fast. About a kilometre up the road, having dropped her cloak by accident or design, she veered off the track and headed south into the fields that marked the ill-defined border between North Canberra and Gungahlin. Realising that they were now well outside their territory, half of her pursuers gave up, and returned to Kaleen.

Three goons of Gungahlin continued to pursue her. Diana was a sprinter, but they were stayers. Bit by bit, on uneven ground with clumps of long grass that made for heavy going, they were catching up on her.

Under these circumstances, of course, a heroine will often stumble and fall, and be at the mercy of whatever malevolent force is bearing down on her. Diana was as nimble of step as she was fleet of foot. But in the semi-darkness, she didn't see the entrance to the rabbit hole until her foot became caught in it, and she went tumbling down.

9. Ill Met by Goonlight

The two newlyweds wandered arm-in-arm through the streets of North Canberra in the moonlight until they reached the home of the Oligarch of O'Connor around midnight. The Oligarch had mixed feelings about their arrival. He was:

a. heartened to see his son Gerald again, or at least relieved that he had not been forcibly married to the Baron's sister, which would have made her the Oligarch's daughter-in-law;
b. surprised to see the Grandee of Giralang, and it pleased him to think that one of the Baron's lieutenants had defected to North Canberra;
c. startled that Gerald and the Grandee were married; but
d. alarmed to learn of his daughter's unorthodox diversionary tactic. She was used to being chased by men, but she had ventured into alien territory.

***

The Oligarch would have been even more concerned if he had known that she had tripped over a rabbit hole, and went tumbling to the ground. When she tried to get up, she found that she couldn't put any weight on her left foot. Three goons of Gungahlin closed in on her. They were the brothers Goon: Drag, Lag, and Nar Nar.

'Well, well, well. What have we here?' cried Drag Goon. 'Looks like we've caught a big bunny rabbit.'

Lag Goon guffawed oafishly, while Nar Nar Goon, a sly dog, started circling round to her right.

'This rabbit can bite,' insisted Diana as she whipped out her hunting knife, the blade of which glinted romantically in the moonlight.

Drag was undeterred. He stood in front of her, arms crossed. Then he signalled Lag to move round to her left. The three of them circled her, moving in ever closer. Diana made one or two quick thrusts with her knife to keep them at bay, but she couldn't keep turning on one leg. She fell over again. The three were about to pounce when a voice rang out behind them.

'Good evening, gentlemen. Nice night for hunting.'

'Yes, isn't it just?' Drag kept his eye on Diana, but Lag turned to face the new arrival, who stood there with Diana's cloak slung over his shoulder. 'Who be you be?'

'I'm her psychiatrist. We have to lock her up whenever there's a full moon. Unfortunately, tonight, she gnawed through the bars of her cell and escaped from the madhouse.' Diana caught his wink, arched her back and howled at the moon.

'You're no cyclist,' said Nar Nar. 'You're Captain Guard.'

'And, at the moment, her guardian.' He tossed Diana her cloak, which she wrapped around her shoulders. 'Now, we don't want a diplomatic incident, do we, gentlemen? Not with the political situation so precariously balanced.'

'You're on our land,' insisted Drag Goon, who turned to face the captain. 'We can take you prisoner as well.'

'Actually,' he replied, 'I think we are on the lands of the Mud

People. And you might have a difficult time explaining to your Governor about fraternising with the guards from Kaleen.'

A short time later, Captain Guard was piggy-backing Diana along the track to the Barton Bridge and North Lyneham. He glanced back once or twice in case the nonplussed Goons had changed their minds (if they had any), and decided to follow them. They did, but kept a safe distance.

'I should be indebted to you,' said Diana, reluctantly.

'Don't sound so enthusiastic,' he panted. Diana was a trim slip of a girl, but surprisingly heavy for her size.

'Would you like me to carry you instead?' she asked, sarcastically.

'Nearly there,' he grunted, as he carried her past the remains of the Barton Bridge, and deposited her on a grassy bank in the moonlight.

'What now?' asked Diana as she adjusted her cloak. She reached down to her ankle. 'I think it's a bit better now. Ow.'

'Evidently not.' He examined it. 'It's badly swollen. I'll take you back to the Grand Duke's house.'

'Really? You're not going to take advantage of me?'

He thought for a moment. Truth to tell, he was not in much of a position to take advantage of anyone. He was a strong, fit man, but, alas, one with a lower back problem. 'Next full moon,' he promised her.

He was about to pick her up again when he heard low voices from the other side of Barton Bridge. Clambering up on the rubble, he listened carefully. The Brothers Goon and the guards of Kaleen were talking.

'That's right, gentlemen,' he called through the rubble. 'You didn't see us, and we didn't see you because we weren't here. Nobody saw anybody and nothing happened.'

He carried Diana as far as Ellen Street before he had to set her down again. It was a shame – a warm night, a full moon, and a beautiful girl – only she had a swollen ankle and his back was starting to spasm.

'What is your first name?' she asked.

'Trex.'

'That's very unusual.'

'It was originally T. Rex. My father was interested in dinosaurs.'

Sometime later, they hobbled into the compound of the Grand Duke of North Lyneham. His light was still on. He didn't look too pleased when he answered the knock on his door. 'I was just about to go to bed,' he complained.

'Sorry, milord,' said Trex. 'I need somewhere for Diana to stay the night. She's sprained her ankle. Perhaps in the morning we could contact the Dowager Duchess of Downer to get one of her herbal ...'

He trailed off. The lady in question emerged from the direction of the bedroom. 'Cossie darling, what is all the fuss about?'

***

All in all, it was a beautiful, warm, moonlit night full of frustrated romantic opportunities. While Trex gave the Grand Duke and visiting Duchess a briefing on the events that had transpired that evening, the Duchess bathed Diana's foot and applied a poultice. Then she kneaded the captain's back, which made him wonder if she was trying to immobilise him.

After that, no one was in the mood for romance, except for Gerald and Algernon. Next day, they were still basking in the afterglow of their nuptials, when Diana, to her great indignity, was wheeled in on a cart. Father was pleased to see her, and so was Gerald.

'Hello, sister dear. Did you have a pleasant journey?'

She growled, and said something unladylike through clenched teeth.

***

While it may have been difficult to catch what Diana said, it would have been a wonder if everyone in Canberra did not hear the blood-curdling wail that emanated from Beth later that day when the Baron broke to her the news of Gerald's escape.

She would have gone on the rampage, wreaking havoc on all wildlife and mildfolk in the vicinity, but the Baron knew how to handle his sister. He punched her on the jaw and knocked her out cold.

The following evening, the citizens of Giralang were again gathering in a park, this time to choose a successor to the Grandee. But the meeting had barely got under way when the Baron turned up with his sister Beth and a party of Beastly Boys.

'Citizens of Giralang. You managed to have your leader kidnapped under your very noses, and no one lifted a finger to help him. You are a pack of gutless wonders who are not capable of governing yourselves. I have therefore chosen your new leader for you. My sister Beth is now the Guardian of Giralang. She will live in the Grandee's house, and choose one of you to be her husband.'

No assembly ever broke up more quickly than that one. The Baron went on his way. On the whole, he was satisfied with the course of events. He didn't really fancy having Gerald as his brother in law; his less than enthusiastic lieutenant, the Grandee of Giralang was gone, and he now had his sister Beth out of his hair.

On his way home, the Baron stopped off to visit the Caliph of Kaleen.

'Diana rescued Gerald and the Grandee rather easily, don't you think?' the Baron remarked.

The Caliph felt uneasy. 'I wouldn't know, effendi.'

'To get back to North Lyneham, they would have had to pass by the edges of your territory, or even through it. Did your guards see nothing?'

'They reported nothing. Of course, Diana is a skilled huntress. She may have slipped past them.'

'But Gerald and the Grandee are not. Those blundering oafs should have been easy to detect, and capture.'

'I–I will check, effendi.'

Next day, the Caliph summoned his three guards and asked them if they had seen anything.

'We didn't see anything,' said the first.

'And nobody saw us,' insisted the second.

'Because they weren't there,' added the third.

'Who weren't there?' asked the Caliph.

'Erm, Diana and Gerald and the Grandee.'

'Really? And who else wasn't there that didn't see you?'

'Well,' replied the second, 'the Goons of Gungahlin.'

'Anyone else?'

'Captain Guard,' added the first. 'Nobody saw anybody and nothing happened.' His two companions nodded in agreement on that point.

The Caliph stroked his chin beard thoughtfully. 'Very well. Dismissed.'

***

Later, on the remains of the road north of the Barton Bridge, the three guards were sharing a flagon with the three Goons and smoking certain substances, when the Caliph turned up. The guards stood up unsteadily, saluted, then withdrew to just off the edge of their side of the road, while the Goons retreated to the other side, which put them back in Gungahlin territory.

'Good evening,' said the Caliph, cheerily. 'It is pleasing to see that fraternal relations have been established with our neighbours in Gungahlin.'

None of them could think of anything clever to say in reply. In fact, they couldn't even think of anything stupid to say.

The Caliph turned his attention to the brothers Goon. 'Tell me, did anything unusual happen the night before last?'

Drag and Nar Nar exchanged uneasy glances, while Lag guffawed. 'I'll say, there was this chick who—'

Drag nudged him in the ribs. 'Nobody saw anybody.'

Nar Nar added, 'and nothing happened.'

'I see.' The Caliph started pacing to and fro. He motioned to the two groups to get back together. 'Please, do not let me restrain your inter-territorial festivities.'

The men looked at each other warily before returning to the roadway.

'In a line, if you please.'

They lined up, wondering what would happen next.

'I would like a volunteer,' said the crafty Caliph. '– someone who is smart and big and bold – for a special mission. Would that volunteer take one step forward, please?'

With a quick exchange of glances, five of the six men stepped back a pace, leaving Lag standing there.

'Excellent.' The Caliph beamed. 'Have I got a deal for you.'

10. Bogans and Bogongs

Lag Goon was a big, dopey fellow, who was puzzled that the Caliph should want him to volunteer for a special mission.

'What's in it for me if I do?' he asked.

'Lust and power.'

The other Goons and the Kaleen guards laughed.

'What does that mean?'

'It means that I want you to capture a woman and ravish her. If you do that, you will be powerful.'

Lag thought for a moment. 'That chick we were chasing the other night?'

The laughter behind him became raucous.

The Caliph grimaced. 'Diana? No. You wouldn't want her, anyway. She's all skin and bone. What you need is a woman with meat.'

***

The following day, it was announced that all bachelors in Giralang were to assemble at the Grandee's house that evening, where their new leader, Elizabeth von Belco, would choose one of them to be her husband.

Lieutenant Shrubsole and Private Underling marched through the streets, calling out, 'Bring out your unwed.'

Some men tried to flee the suburb, but guards were waiting for them and herded them back. Others resorted to proposing marriage to the nearest available unattached female, or to each other, at least for a short term engagement, in the hope that this would render them ineligible.

In the meantime, the Baron rounded up the Prelate of Page and told him that he had to perform a marriage ceremony that evening.

'Who are the lucky couple?'

'My sister Beth is getting married.'

'To whom?'

'We don't know yet. We'll find out tonight.'

***

That evening, Lieutenant Shrubsole was quaking in his boots when he reported to the Baron. 'I don't understand it, sir,' he explained as he swatted away a moth. 'I thought there were plenty of eligible men in Giralang, but they all seem to be engaged, or have disappeared.'

'Hmm.' The Baron was about to speak when a moth hit him in the face. His sister guffawed. It was the annual invasion of the Bogong moths, and the air was soon thick with them.

'Lieutenant Shrubsole,' asked the Baron. 'Does that include your guards?'

'Sir?'

'Are any of your guards still single?'

There was a deadly hush, broken only by the whir of moth wings. The Baron paced up and down in front of Shrubsole and his nervous troops. 'Well? Speak up.'

Shrubsole gathered his guards together for a quick confab. 'One of you beggars is going to have to volunteer. I know some of you are single, or at least, not legally married. Now, which one will it be?'

Soon after, there was a yelp, and Shrubsole dragged out a thin weed of a man.

The Baron grinned. 'Ah, Private Underling. Did you just volunteer?'

'No sir. Lieutenant Shrubsole pinched my ear, sir.'

The other men laughed nervously, but Beth looked at Underling disdainfully. 'I don't want him. There's no meat on him.'

Private Underling felt both elated and deflated: elated that the world's ugliest woman didn't want him, and deflated by the thought that if she didn't fancy him, who on earth would?

'Then,' asked the Baron in exasperation, 'who do you want?'

Beth pointed to a burley fellow approaching the gathering. He was wearing a pair of stubbies and a check shirt. She loved the manly way he was catching the Bogong moths and stuffing them into his gob. 'I want that one.'

The Baron peered at him. 'Who are you?'

'My name is Lag Goon,' said the fellow slowly, after spitting out some moth wings. 'I have come to capture and ravish some chick named Beth.'

Everyone stared at him in astonishment, except for Beth, who cried, 'Take me! Take me!'

It was love at first sight; Beth and Lag rushed towards each other. Forget about Heathcliff and what's-her-name running along the Wuthering Heights: think of two rhinos charging, or hippopotami, or even elephants.

What happened next was quite unseemly and best left to your imagination. Come to think of it, you probably wouldn't want to imagine it at all.

'Padre,' called the Baron.

The Prelate stood on the sidelines, not knowing where to look. Only a sense of morbid fascination caused him to take a peek at the discomfiting spectacle. The Baron's Beastly Boys, however, had no such inhibitions, and were cheering and urging the cumbersome couple on.

'Do your duty,' insisted the Baron.

'Really, this is most irregular.'

'Just do it.'

Nervously, he approached the cavorting couple and intoned, 'Do you, er, whatever your name is, take this woman to be—'

'Skip that bit. They obviously do.'

'By the powers vested in me under the Marriage Act of Canberra, I now pronounce you man and wife. You may kiss the bride. Oh, you already are.'

The men cheered, probably in relief, except for Private Underling, who fainted.

Later, the newlyweds prepared a wedding feast, by plucking moths out of the air and tossing them on a fire to roast them. 'Plenty of meat on a moth,' said Beth. They washed them down with a flagon of fermented substances.

But Beth wanted 'a real, proper wedding, with a white dress and bridesmaids and things'. Their parents having died or disowned them long ago, the Baron had to provide for his sister's wedding. He arranged it for a fortnight hence. A large, whitish dress was made, possibly out of an old tent. Two girls were dragooned into being bridesmaids – speaking of which – Drag Goon was best man and Nar Nar Goon piped in the bride on his nose flute.

This time, the bewildered Prelate was able to perform a proper wedding ceremony. Lag placed a curtain ring, which he assured Beth was finest quality brass, on her podgy finger. Beth cried, or at least produced a collection of sighs and snorts, which sounded like a hippopotamus having a fit of hysteria.

The Caliph and his guards were in attendance. 'Excellency,' said the Caliph to the Baron. 'News of this wedding travelled to North Canberra.' He handed the Baron a scroll. 'This was attached to an arrow that was fired over the GDE at Ellen Bridge this morning.'

It was a letter of felicitations to the happy couple, signed by such dignitaries as the Tyrant of Turner, the Grand Duke of North Lyneham, the Dowager Duchess of Downer, the Oligarch of O'Connor and his daughter Diana, his son Gerald and his son-in-law Algernon (formerly the Grandee of Giralang) and Captain Trex Guard.

'Very touching,' said the Baron. He nodded towards Lag. 'Where did you dig him up?'

'The Goons often fraternise with my guards,' explained the Caliph. 'Since we want to encourage good relations with Gungahlin, I thought he would be a suitable choice.'

'He is indeed. My one regret is that my sister is now called Beth von Goon. Still, to get her out of my hair, I wouldn't have cared if she married the Man in the Moon.'

'In that case,' retorted the Caliph, 'she would be Beth von Moon.'

***

Earlier that day, Diana had fired the arrow with the message over the embankment. She was watched by Captain Guard, who asked, 'how is the ankle, milady?'

'It has recovered. I can now run like the wind again. How is your back?'

'Much better.' He looked up at the sky. 'New Moon tonight.'

Diana knew what that meant. In two weeks' time, there would be a full moon, and he would come hunting for her.

11. The Governor of Gungahlin

As he sat in his office, Percival Gerontius V, Governor of Gungahlin, gazed at the portraits on the wall. His predecessors were there and they all looked much the same – firm jawed and steely-eyed, they radiated an aura of calm, but strict authority.

They seemed to be watching him to make sure he would meet their exacting standards. The problem was that it was unrealistic to think that down through the generations, their successors could all have those same commanding looks. Percival Gerontius V had a middle-aged paunch and double chins. His eyes were much softer.

His forebears had all been tough, even ruthless men. While other parts of Canberra had fragmented into local communities, the Governors had insisted on keeping their domain together.

As the population declined, they moved people from the outer suburbs to concentrate them on either side of Gungahlin Drive, in the fortified village of Palmerston and the Gungahlin Town Centre itself. Gin Creek and the chain of ponds running alongside Gun Road to the north had been set aside for irrigation and crops, while the lands to the south down to Sullivan's Creek were used for grazing, or for broad acre, low yield grain crops.

As the outer suburbs were abandoned, their houses were systematically stripped of anything that could be of value, especially metal, glass and plastic. These were stockpiled and recycled, or traded for food because the lands between the two creeks were often dry and yielded little produce.

Most valuable of all had been the southern outpost at Mitchell, an old industrial centre from which had been extracted the bodies of many ancient transport vehicles – themselves a goldmine of metal, glass and plastic. There were also disused tile and concrete factories, furniture stores and even electrical appliances.

Nearby was Goon Farm. It had once been the city's cemetery and crematorium, so the land was unusually fertile. From there, the Governor's guards could patrol the borders with Belco to the west and the Mud People to the south.

But Percival Gerontius V was not in the mood to contemplate such things. He was wondering if he could get rid of his paunch and his double chin. He could try dieting, but it would look bad if the governor at least did not eat well.

His reverie was interrupted when Cyril Suckling, his Executive Assistant, breezed in. Descended from a long line of ministerial advisors, who had adapted to the decline in governments and ministers by attaching themselves to other persons of authority, Cyril was a deeply ingrained mixture of over-confidence, officiousness and obsequiousness.

'Good morning, sir. How are we?' he asked with irritating cheerfulness.

'I am well.' Percival saw a papyrus in Suckling's hand. 'What little problems do we have to deal with today?'

'There are three of them, I'm afraid. And not necessarily little.'

The Governor groaned inwardly. Dealing with one simple problem was often hard enough. 'And what are these not necessarily little problems?'

'Lag Goon has married Beth von Belco.'

'The acting Grandee of Giralang?'

'Yes. Although the Caliph of Kaleen is rumoured to be planning to add Giralang to his domains.'

'Much joy may it bring him.' Percival thought for a moment. 'Lag Goon is hardly a loss to us, is he? He may be physically large, but he is no intellectual giant.'

'True,' Cyril conceded. 'But if he and Beth have children, the Baron may use them as a pretext to claim Goon Farm, and annex it to his territories. Apart from the loss of fertile land, it could be used as a springboard from which to attack Mitchell.'

'Oh, dear.'

'Fortunately, that is cancelled out by the second problem, but complicated by the third.'

'You speak in riddles, Cyril.'

Cyril showed him the piece of papyrus. 'I've just received word from the manager of our scrap mine at Mitchell that there is no more scrap to be extracted. Every skerrick of metal, glass, plastic or anything else that might be useful has now been exhausted.'

Percival could see the inevitable consequence. 'Then all we can do is to keep recycling the material we already have.'

'Yes, but there are problems. We have recycled the metal so much that most of it has rusted away. Many of our solar panels are turning into rust buckets.'

'Well, can we extract the metal from the rust?'

'That would be difficult. Most of it crumbles into the soil as iron oxide.'

The Governor put his head in his hands. 'Then what are we to do?'

Cyril shrugged his shoulders. 'We shall have to find new sources of metal.'

'And what about the third problem?'

'I have heard a rumour that the Grand Wizard has suggested that the Wazir of Watson should annex the territory of the Mud People.'

'Why?'

'Apparently the Wizard believes that the Mud People have been self-contained for too long, and are in danger of inbreeding. He has also warned that in a generation or two, we may face a similar problem.'

'Everyone related to everyone else?' The Governor pondered this for a moment. Most people in Gungahlin were related to each other in some way. When he thought of the Brothers Goon, he realised that inbreeding may already have started. 'That's all very well, but why should it concern us?'

'If the Wazir annexes the Mud People, and the Baron takes control of Goon Farm and Mitchell, our southern borders are compromised. Any subsequent fighting between Belco and North Canberra could spill over into our lands.'

'What would you have us do? Annex the Mud People ourselves?'

Cyril nodded. 'As a pre-emptive measure. It would also give us the advantage of interbreeding with their gene pool.'

'To our mutual advantage?'

'Yes, although the Mud People aren't as inbred as the Grand Wizard thinks. He evidently doesn't know that they trade more than spuds. They ferment them to produce a brew called sly grog, which they sell in shanties on the Feral Highway. Those shanties are also where some of their ladies offer certain services to the male patrons. I'm sure they've interbred with the North Canberrans and our people more than the Grand Wizard realises.' Cyril paused. 'There is, however, a cultural problem.'

'A cultural problem?'

'The Mud People have become devotees of a cult that maintains that they are the chosen people. One day, they will be led to a land of milk and honey known as Wagga Bay.'

The Governor frowned in puzzlement. 'Wagga Bay? There was an old town called Wagga, long since abandoned, but that was inland from here.'

'It was indeed. But the Mud People are a fusion of the Sea People, who came from coastal districts, and the Dirt People who came from inland towns like Wagga. Somehow, their two histories have become mixed up with each other.'

The Governor sighed. 'So they're a bunch of geographically confused sly grog harlots with religious mania?'

'Eloquently put, sir.'

***

Percival Gerontius V stared out over his domain. He could now see what it had never occurred to him to notice until Cyril pointed it out. Many of the solar panels were rusting; window panes were cracked or boarded up; plastic was brittle and faded. None of this was due to a corrosive atmosphere. Just age, sheer age, and the heat.

He wondered if his people would still have the skills to mine for metal, refine it and work it into shape. Did any of them know how to blow glass? As for plastic, how could one make any without petrochemicals?

Now Cyril wanted him to invade the Mud People. He couldn't see it working, somehow. His troops, such as they were, lacked the skills and aggression to be warriors. They hadn't fought anybody for ages. Perhaps he could play off the Baron von Belco against the Wazir of Watson. If one threatened his land, he could appeal to the other.

Percival spent an agitated morning, but as the torpor of the afternoon set in, he decided that the best thing to do was nothing. He wanted to enjoy the rich, warm balm of complacency while it lasted.

***

A few days later, Cyril had some startling news for him. 'It's Beth von Belco, sir. She's defected to us and moved with her husband to Goon Farm.'

'Oh.' Percival wasn't sure how to react to this.

'It seems she's always wanted to be a chicken wrangler.'

'A what?'

'She probably means a chicken strangler. Apparently, she enjoys killing things.'

Percival blanched. 'Has there been any reaction from the Baron?'

'He is reputed to have said "good riddance" under his breath.'

'Well,' said Governor Gerontius, rubbing his hands with glee. 'That solves one problem. So, who is in control of Giralang now?'

'The Caliph of Kaleen is now the Caliph of Kalang.'

'Really? He will soon be powerful enough to rival the Baron.'

Cyril nodded. 'If he does, he'll be ten times as dangerous. Unlike the Baron, he does actually have some brains.'

'We'll cross that bridge when we come to it,' Percival retorted. 'Now, I have some news for you. The Mayor of the Mud People has requested a meeting.'

12. The Battle of O'Connor Ridge

Baron von Belco was hot and bothered. Beads of sweat were forming on his florid face as he waited for his lieutenants to arrive. He was standing by the Great Owl on the corner of Benway and Belcoway.

It was a religious site, which didn't bother the Baron in the least. It was the centre of a cult, where the devotees of the Great Wise Owl met from time to time to pray for deliverance from Gaia's Curse, or from toothache or anything else that was bothering them. There were similar cults centred on other statues all around Canberra. The ancients had built them centuries earlier. Purpose: unknown.

Who knows that the ancients thought? the Baron mused to himself. If the statues were meant to appease the gods, then, given the disasters that had befallen the world, they hadn't done a very good job.

The Caliph of Kalang and the Archon of Aranda arrived together. Were they conspiring against the Baron? 'Effendi.' Bowing, the Caliph gave an extravagant hand gesture.

Crawler, thought the Baron. The Caliph was getting too big for his boots. The Archon merely gave a polite nod.

'The reason I have called you here today,' explained the Baron, 'is to plan the next phase of our campaign.' His lieutenants looked at each other uneasily. 'Now that we have the tunnel through the GDE at Belcoway, we should use it.'

'Effendi, we tried that once,' the Caliph replied. 'With disastrous consequences.'

'Not really,' the Baron retorted. 'We captured the Oligarch of O'Connor's son.'

'Yes, but then Diana rescued him, and we lost the Grandee of Giralang.'

'Much to your advantage,' the Baron reminded him.

'But, Excellency,' the Archon said. 'Capturing Gerald was the merest chance. Otherwise, our forces were routed. Why should we be more successful with a second attack?'

'Because, if we do it at night, we will have the element of surprise.'

'But how will we see in the dark?' protested the Caliph.

'In three night's time, there will be a full moon,' explained the Baron. 'So have your troops ready by then.'

***

Next day, Percival Gerontius, Governor of Gungahlin, had a visitor: the Mayor of the Mud People.

The Mayor was a short, swarthy, thickset man with shifty eyes and a sly voice. When Cyril Suckling ushered him into the Governor's office, he looked around uneasily.

'To what do we owe the pleasure of this visit, Your Worship?' asked Percival.

'Worship? Yes, very probably.' The Mayor's voice was little more than a loud whisper. Percival and Cyril exchanged glances. They wondered if the Mayor was quite right in the head. Suddenly, his eyes stopped darting back and forth and he stared straight at Percival. 'I need an ally.'

Percival blinked. 'Don't we all?'

'Between the Wazir of Watson and the Baron, we are facing common threats,' said Cyril.

'Common threats? Yess,' hissed the Mayor, then added under his breath, 'very common.'

'Pardon?' asked Percival.

'It's my wife,' admitted the Mayor. 'I want to be rid of her.'

'Eh?'

'She's a nuisance. And she questions our holy writ. I want someone to kidnap her.'

'What about the Wazir or the Baron?'

'I'm asking you first. We could make it look like one of them did it.'

Percival looked at Cyril before replying. 'Your Worship, we have a policy of non-intervention in the affairs of others, a policy that has served us well for many …'

Percival trailed off. The Mayor was staring at the wall. 'What is that?'

'That is a map of New South Wales. Cyril found it in the basement the other day. It's in surprisingly good condition, considering it must be hundreds of years old.'

There was a gleam in the Mayor's eyes as he went over to examine it. 'All my life, I have wanted to see such a thing. Show me, where is Wagga Bay?'

***

'Now look what you've done,' complained Percival after they had restrained the gibbering wreck of the Mayor, who, on discovering Wagga was actually inland, went berserk. They'd had to call in guards to restrain him and take him off to the cells.

'Me?' asked Cyril innocently.

'You were the one who insisted that we put that map on the wall.'

'I thought he would appreciate it.'

Percival shook his head. 'You knew he would see where Wagga really was, and go mad.'

'He was mad anyway. But now, we can legitimately restrain him for conspiracy to kidnap and causing an affray.'

'When news gets out that we have arrested their Mayor, the Mud People will attack.'

Cyril nodded. 'However, their force is so puny, we are bound to beat them.'

'Not if they get themselves allies – the Wazir or the Baron.'

Cyril nodded again. 'Which is why we must attack first, before the Mud People can get any allies. I believe it is called a pre-emptive strike.'

Governor Gerontius stared at his executive assistant in horror. Cyril Suckling was turning into a monster.

***

A full moon in spring, and a young man's thoughts turn to lust. Trex Guard had promised to hunt Diana that night, to capture her and to have his wicked way with her. Of course, being a gentleman, he had given her warning that if she went out that night, she knew what, or who, to expect.

Nor did he want to stalk her, at least, not in the vicinity of her father's house. In the early evening, he took up a position a few hundred metres away, in the clearing at the top of a hill in a patch of woodland, from where he could see the house.

A clear, warm night, and the moon arose. Never had he seen such a glorious golden globe. It was bigger and brighter than ever. Or maybe it was just that his senses were heightened. It shone on his clearing, on the house of the Oligarch of O'Connor, and on the disparate desperados gathering on Belcoway, to the west of the GDE.

'This is exciting, isn't it?' said Private Underling. 'A moonlit midnight adventure.'

'If you say so,' replied Lieutenant Shrubsole, who could think of better ways to spend a warm, moonlit night. Hearing the sound of singing, he looked along the road to where a column of troops were marching:

With hobnail boots, we trample on our foes
With hobnail boots, we stomp on all their toes.
'Company, halt,' barked Sergeant Owwible.

A familiar figure turned up, with a new stick. 'Right, men,' said the Baron. 'This is what we're going to do. We're going to launch a raid on the Oligarch of O'Connor. We will go through the tunnel and march to the fork in the road.

'Then we'll split into two groups. The Caliph's group will take the left fork and attack the Oligarch's place from the north. The Archon and I shall take the rest of the troops further along Belcoway, then attack from the south. Silence is essential.'

'Isn't he supposed to ask if we have any questions?' asked Underling, quietly. Shrubsole merely glared at him.

So the men tried to make their way through the dark crevices of the tunnel they had fashioned earlier. Fortunately, the Caliph had the sense to bring a stave, which he lit. Once the men had scrambled through, they marched up the road towards their destiny.

***

It must have been about nine in the evening when Trex Guard saw a shadowy figure emerge from the Archon's house. Diana! His heart missed a beat. He had never felt this way about a girl before. He knew that if he captured her, it would be for keeps.

For her part, Diana had guessed where he might be waiting for her. She enjoyed the thrill of the chase, whether being the hunter or the hunted. She decided to spiral her way up the hill, and take him by surprise.

***

'This is the way we came through last time,' Lieutenant Shrubsole told the Caliph.

'Are you sure?'

Shrubsole nodded. 'The clearing where we found Gerald is just up ahead.'

'But where is the Oligarch's house?'

'Somewhere nearby, I suppose.'

'Should we ask for directions?' suggested Private Underling.

The Caliph frowned at him. 'Do you think we can accost a stranger in the dark and say: Excuse me, we're an invading army. Which is the way to your leader's house?'

Shrubsole pointed through a gap in the trees. 'There's a light down there, sir. That could be the Oligarch's house.'

The Caliph looked up at the stars. The light was aligned with the Southern Cross. 'Well, it is to the south.'

So the Caliph and his band turned to the south, and headed past the clearing. As they did so, Private Underling had the strange feeling they were being followed.

***

'How much further?' asked the Baron of the Archon, as they marched along Belcoway.

'Difficult to say,' replied the Archon. 'My map is too faded to make sense by moonlight.'

'There are some lights over to the left,' observed Sergeant Owwible.

'Then let's try over there.' The Baron led his men off the road and into the trees. It might have been romantic, wandering around in the scrub in the moonlight, but it was soon clear they had no idea where they were going.

***

In the clearing, Trex Guard could hear movement in the bushes to the west. Was Diana trying to circle him? He decided to creep up behind her. But when he did so, he was puzzled. She was making too much noise. Was she trying to entice him? Then he heard muffled voices. Something was wrong.

Diana, meanwhile, circled her way up to the clearing. When she got there, it was deserted. What to do? Perhaps he hadn't arrived yet. She decided to retrace her steps.

***

'Sorry, sir. We can't see a damned thing,' complained Sergeant Owwible as he tripped over another mallee root.

The Baron peered into the semi-gloom. The moonlight filtering through the shadows of the trees made distances difficult to judge. 'There's a clearing up there. You and the men stay here until I signal to you.'

***

Trex Guard tensed and listened. Someone was coming up the hill, and not very silently either. He couldn't see the shape clearly, but it had to be Diana. He waited until they walked past him, then reached out to grope them. Funny! Diana was a lot chunkier that he thought she was.

The figure turned round sharply. Two faces stared at each other in the moonlight. Two voices let out mighty roars. The Baron and Trex reached for their sticks.

***

'Our fearless leader is in trouble,' shouted Sergeant Owwible. 'Chee-arge!'

***

Private Underling, who had been sent on ahead to reconnoitre, came stumbling back and fell in front of the Caliph. 'Enemy approaching, sir.'

The Caliph nodded to Lieutenant Shrubsole, who cried, 'Right lads. Up and at 'em.'

***

Diana watched in astonishment as two bands of grown men got stuck into each other in the scrub on the moonlit hillside. Some sparred with staves while others resorted to fisticuffs.

Cut off from her home, she couldn't get back to warn her father of what was happening, although it was likely that the war cries and howls of pain would reach his ears anyway. She headed back up the hill to the clearing, where she saw Trex and the Baron duelling in the moonlight. Trex was the more dexterous wielder of his stick, but the Baron was the more powerful man.

Stringing her bow, she took an arrow from her quiver, and waited her chance. Trex stumbled and fell back. The Baron bore down on him. Diana fired her arrow at his rump.

For a second or two, the Baron didn't seem to notice. Then he uttered a blood curdling cry, and dashed off into the undergrowth.

Trex lay there panting as Diana towered over him.

'Gosh. That was exciting,' she said. Then she leapt on top of him.

13. The Mud People

The Battle of O'Connor Ridge was one of the most embarrassing events in the annals of military history. Almost unbeknownst to the local inhabitants, two groups of an invading force had entered their domain, fought a pitched battle with each other in the scrub, and then withdrawn.

It was the Archon's bald pate glistening in the moonlight, and the distinctive shape of the Caliph's turban, that caused both leaders to recognise each other after several minutes of fighting. They shouted to their men to withdraw, whereupon they shot off into the scrub. There were shouts and cries as they ran into each other in the bushes. Fortunately, Sergeant Owwible and Lieutenant Shrubsole had loud enough voices that they were able to order their men back to the roads.

The two groups nearly came to blows again when they reached the fork in the road. Once they had sorted themselves out, they limped in orderly fashion towards the GDE. They stopped when they heard a wild animal bellowing as it crashed through the undergrowth.

Lieutenant Shrubsole drew his commander aside. 'I've heard tell that there used to be a lion park at a town called Double.'

'Double what?' asked the Caliph.

'Double lions, I suppose. Legend has it that when the park was shut down because of the economy collapsing, the lions escaped.'

The Caliph listened carefully. 'It sounds like a wounded bull to me.'

Moments later, a wild beast crashed out of the bushes and onto the road in front of them.

'Get this thing out of me,' roared the Baron, as he tried pulling the arrow from his rump.

When the troops saw the Baron's plight, they tittered. Then they chuckled. Then they fell about in hysterical laughter.

'Sergeant Owwible,' called the Caliph.

'Sah.' The Sergeant had tears streaming from his eyes.

'Lie down, Baron,' ordered the Caliph. 'Lieutenant Shrubsole, you hold him down. Sergeant, you're probably the strongest man here. You can pull out the arrow.'

Lieutenant Shrubsole held the Baron's legs while Sergeant Owwible grabbed hold of the arrow. 'Tough little blighter.'

'Pull, pull, pull,' chanted the men.

'If I give it a little jiggle … Ah, gotcha.'

The men cheered. The Baron let out a mighty roar. There were tears in his eyes, partly because of the pain, but mainly because he knew he would never live this down.

It wasn't long before he would be known as Rumplestiltskin.

***

It is said that two people can look out through the same bars, with one seeing the mud and the other, the stars. The Mayor of the Mud People saw, well, not mud exactly, but dry, dusty ground in the moonlight.

He was in the depths of despair. Not only had he been captured by the heathen, but they had tried his faith by showing him a map of New South Wales: Wagga had been an inland town.

Where, then, was Wagga Bay? Ah, he had it! Wagga Bay existed, not as an actual place, but as an idea in the hearts and minds of the Mud People. All they had to do was to march to the coast, find a place that suited their purpose, and declare it to be Wagga Bay.

He was entertaining this prospect when a sheet of paper was slipped under his door. He stared at it incredulously. It was a map of the ancient town of Wagga, with one road branching off towards the river, and a caption saying Wagga Wagga Beach Caravan Park.

So, there was a Wagga Beach, not by the sea, but on the banks of the Budgie River. (The river originally had a much longer name, which had been shortened and corrupted over time.)

'Wagga Beach,' he muttered to himself, thoughtfully.

There was the sound of a key turning in the lock of his cell door. Then silence. Had they forgotten to lock the door when they'd fed him earlier? He tried the handle and the door opened. He peered out into a courtyard. There was a guard, but he was over in the corner, wrapped in an amorous embrace with a lady.

The Mayor snuck out the other way, onto the street. He could hardly believe his luck. There was a bicycle leaning against a post. On closer inspection, it looked like his. He wasn't going to argue. He hopped on the bike and gleefully rode away in the moonlight.

***

The Mayor might not have been so gleeful if he had known what was happening back at his home in EPIC. Jemima, his wife, was an earthy woman, who had married her husband more out of economic necessity than desire. She was eagerly waiting for the figure who clambered up on to the balcony.

'Wazza, darling, so glad you could come.'

The Wazir of Watson, whose name was Warren, was an oily little man who had a certain hypnotic charm. He put a finger to his lips. 'Shh. I don't want my wives to know I am here.'

'Wives? How many have you got?'

'Just the three.' He took her in his arms. 'But a man needs some variety.'

Jemima giggled. She was about to lead him into the bedroom when she saw a familiar figure cycle into the courtyard. 'Oh, my God. It's my husband.'

'I thought he was in prison.'

'He must have escaped.' They heard the front door open. 'He's very jealous. Quick. Get onto the roof until the coast is clear.'

So the Wazir of Watson climbed onto the roof and waited in the moonlight. Hopefully, Jemima would exercise her charms on her husband to distract him while the Wazir made his getaway. But the Mayor kept going on excitedly about a place called Wagga Beach, which was apparently the Promised Land.

The Wazir knew he was in for a long wait.

***

The Oligarch of O'Connor and his folk had heard strange cries and crashing around in the undergrowth. He asked his Captain of the Guard, Sergeant Beefy, whether perhaps he (Sergeant Beefy, that is) ought to investigate. The Sergeant replied that perhaps he ought not.

'Whatever it is, it doesn't seem to be getting any closer. I think we're better off taking up defensive positions here.'

In the quiet of the morning, he went out with his guards to investigate. In the meantime, news of the ructions the night before had reached the Tyrant of Turner, who arrived with some of his troops.

Soon afterwards, Sergeant Beefy returned with three bedraggled individuals, who had spent the night out in the scrub.

'Hello, father,' said Diana.

'Diana. You're safe,' said the Oligarch with obvious relief.

'Hello, father,' said Trex.

'What have you been up to, my boy?' asked the Tyrant. The young couple grinned sheepishly. 'On second thoughts, there is no need to explain.'

The third figure was a miserable little man with tears running down his bloodstained face. 'Woe is me,' he cried.

'Who are you?' asked the Tyrant.

At that moment, Gerald and the Grandee turned up. 'Private Underling, isn't it?' asked the Grandee.

'Yes, sir. We were supposed to capture you, or rescue you. I can't remember which, but things went horribly wrong.'

'Hmm. I think we'd better take him to the herbalist to get his wounds tended to,' said the Tyrant. 'He can explain what happened later.'

***

In fact, Private Underling wasn't able to explain much more than he had already told his captors, because he was as confused as they were about what happened. They decided to leave him in the custody of the herbalist, who was applying salves to his bruises.

'Ooh. A captive man,' she said. 'What I've always wanted.'

'You'd be the first woman that's ever wanted me,' he said, hopefully. 'Ouch. That stings.'

'Never mind, dearie. It's for your own good, er, what is your name?'

'Cecil,' said the little man sadly. 'Cecil Underling.'

'That's a nice name. But if you don't mind me saying so, you don't seem to have the build to be a soldier.'

'I know. When I was a boy, everyone called me sissy Cecil, so I joined the militia to prove them wrong.'

'And did you?'

'Not really,' he admitted. 'What is your name?'

'Deirdre, dearie.' She sighed. 'When I was a girl, everyone called me Dreary Deirdre, so I became a herbalist to prove I could be interesting.'

The thought occurred to Cecil Underling that if he played his cards right, being beaten up, captured, and then held prisoner by a lady herbalist might be the best thing that could happen to him. 'Deirdre. That's a nice name.'

***

Trex and Diana walked hand in hand as they accompanied the Tyrant of Turner back to his house. They were so engrossed in each other that they didn't really care what other people thought when they saw them together.

'Hello, dear,' said Mrs Tyrant as she gave her husband a peck on the cheek. 'Hello, Trex. Hello, Diana.'

'How did you know my name?' asked the young huntress in surprise.

'Trex has casually mentioned your name and described what you were like, at least a dozen times. Judging by what he told us, I'd say you were meant for each other.'

Diana then did something she'd probably never done before. She blushed.

***

'Where have you been?' demanded wife #1 as the Wazir limped into his quarters the following morning.

'You haven't been unfaithful to us, have you?' accused wife #2.

'Oh, you poor dear,' fussed wife #3. 'Have you sprained your ankle?'

'I have been gathering intelligence,' replied the Wazir, smugly. 'Soon, we will be able to annex the Mud People, and their sly grog trade and other, er, services, will be under our control.'

14. New Ideas

A motley band of several hundred souls left EPIC to haul carts and wagons up Flemington Road while singing 'Onward to Wagga Beach.' Some of the lines didn't rhyme, however, because the song was originally 'Onward to Wagga Bay'. It had an odd sort of beat in any case, and lots of incoherent shouting and screaming. It was apparently derived from a primitive form of music known as Rock and Roll. It was believed that rock music went back to the days of the cavemen.

When the procession reached Gungahlin, Governor Percival Gerontius and his Executive Assistant, Cyril Suckling, wished them well and waved them goodbye. In private, Cyril had a quiet chuckle. His plans to annex the Mud People seemed to be going well. It was he who had slipped a copy of an old map of the Wagga Wagga Beach Caravan Park under the Mayor's cell door, and paid Hermione Brimstone to keep the guard occupied while the Mayor had made his escape.

He was not surprised that only about half of the Mud People were leaving. The rest had decided to stay behind because they were more interested in growing potatoes, selling grog or providing intimate services than in some ancient prophecy about their ancestral homelands. They included Jemima, the Mayor's wife, because she said that somebody had to look after the cat.

It was all going as Cyril had hoped. His next step was to pitch his cap for Jemima, the new Mayor of the Mud People, and to become her consort.

Alas, he was not as nimble at climbing balconies to ladies' boudoirs as the wily Wazir of Watson. It wasn't long before Jemima became the Wazir's fourth wife, and the territory of Watson expanded to include EPIC and the potato fields.

***

The Baron von Belco, a.k.a. Rumplestiltskin, had been discredited after the military fiasco at O'Connor. His lieutenants, the Caliph of Kalang and the Archon of Aranda gave him a wide berth for a few days. Eventually, with some trepidation, they called at his house.

They knocked. There was no answer. They asked his neighbours, who said that they saw the Baron limp off the day before, carrying a backpack and heading towards the west.

The Caliph rubbed his hands with glee. 'It seems we are now in control. We could divide Belco between us, if I take the lands north of Belcoway and you take those to the south.'

The Archon thought for a moment. He knew that neither of them was inclined to using military power. 'I think it better if Belco remains united, either under one leader or a governing council, perhaps, ultimately, elected by the people.'

'By the people?' The Caliph seemed incredulous.

'That is how it was done in the old days, before our titles became hereditary and the Baron took over. But for now, I suggest that you be leader, and set up a governing council of community leaders, myself included.'

'Very well.' The two men shook hands on that deal. The Caliph decided not to adopt the Baron's title. It had too many bad connotations.

'And I think we should mend our relations with North Canberra,' added the Archon.

'I agree.' The Caliph knew that the Kaleenites were already friendly with the North Lynehamites.

'I also think that we should deploy our secret weapon.'

'What is that?'

'Trade.'

***

They set the Baron's Beastly Boys to work doing something they were rather good at: demolition. They pulled down the crumbling remains of what had once been Belco's mighty shopping centre to turn it into a large market place for produce from the surrounding suburbs. It was coming in from as far afield as the Fiefdom of Fraser and the Desert of Dunlop. Nor was it long before the products of the Mud People were also finding their way to the Belco markets.

Everybody benefited, except for Cyril Suckling, who had been well and truly trumped. How could he stage a coup to overthrow the Governor of Gungahlin if he did not have the pretext of an external threat? He would have to find some other way to rise to the top.

As for the Baron von Belco, he retreated to the Brindabellas.

***

Norman the Grand Wizard of Siro and Maya the High Priestess of Anu were having one of their regular get-togethers one languid summer afternoon.

'Summers don't seem to be as hot as they used to be,' remarked Maya. 'Bit of a shame, really.'

'Why? It means that slowly but surely, Gaia's Curse is being lifted, and things are getting back to normal.'

'That's the problem. When things were really bad, people had no choice but to pool their resources and help each other out. Now that things are getting better, they're starting to fight each other again.'

Norman nodded. 'Once we were a world, then a nation, then a region, and finally a lot of little communities. Now the communities are reforming into districts – eight of them, probably, since the Mud People are being absorbed into North Canberra. There's bound to be some conflict as that happens.'

Maya nodded. 'That's what worries me.'

'Oh, I don't know. Living in small communities can be secure and comforting, but it can also cause stagnation. Something has got to keep the human race stirred up. Otherwise, where are great new ideas going to come from?'

***

Great new ideas were what Crispin VII craved at that time. The reports coming in to the House On The Hill were not encouraging. Everywhere, the material infrastructure of the city was disintegrating. Metal, glass and plastic had been recycled so often that they were breaking down. New supplies were urgently needed.

Summoning his entourage, he rode in the Presidential surrey out to the east of Burley Griffin to visit Queen Doris of Queanbeyan. He asked if she had any miners.

'Yes we do,' retorted the Queen. 'Nasty pests. They drive out all the native birds.'

'Not Mynahs, miners. People, mainly men who dig holes in the ground.'

'What for?'

'To get out minerals, or stones for building, or sand for glass making.'

'Oh, dear. Now let me think.' She remained silent for a while. 'Sorry. What was the question again?'

***

Quentin, the Karabar Khan was a solidly built young man, like the Baron von Belco, except that he was fair-haired and had a 'baby face'. This caused people to dub him 'the Karabar Kid', which annoyed him almost as much as being called Quentin.

While the President was chatting with the Queen, Quentin was drilling his troops in the showground nearby: 'Left wheel … Right wheel … About face.' He was very good at that sort of thing. But he soon noticed that his troops were losing their coordination. They were distracted by something, or someone.

It was not unusual for their parades to have an audience, something which he and they enjoyed. Standing on the sidelines, shading herself with a parasol, was Jezebel, Begum of Jerra. Even dressed as demurely as she was, she still managed to turn heads. When she batted her eyelids at him, Quentin's heart was all aflutter.

'Hello, Quentin,' said Jezebel.

'Ma'am.' Quentin gave her a fancy salute.

'Impressive,' said Jezebel. 'Most impressive. And so manly, too.'

Quentin puffed out his chest with pride.

'I wish my militia was as good as yours.'

'I believe mine are the finest in the land,' boasted Quentin.

'I don't doubt that. As for mine, well I'm afraid I'm just a poor, helpless female that doesn't know much about military matters.' Jezebel fluttered her eyelids again. 'What my troops need is a man's firm hand.'

Jezebel's looks had been known to make young men swoon. Quentin's baby face was flushed. 'Well, ma'am, perhaps I and my men could help. A bit of drill work, you know.'

'I'm sure you could.' Jezebel locked her arm with his, and they walked. 'I'm sure we could come to some arrangement. Perhaps we could discuss this over dinner at my place.' Quentin couldn't believe his luck. But there is no fool quite like a young fool.

***

On his way back to the House On The Hill, Crispin stopped to speak to the King of Kingston. He was one of those fellows that was genial and doughty at the same time.

'There used to be sand mining in Canberra,' explained the King. 'We had a glass works here. And a shot tower for making lead balls. All gone now, I'm afraid.'

'I don't know if we need any lead balls,' replied Crispin.

'Not unless you're planning to install cannons on Capitol Hill,' joked the King. 'But glassmaking…yes, we could do with more glass. I'll ask some of my subjects and see if they know anything about it. You could ask the Nabob of Narrabundah as well.'

'If I can find him.' Crispin winced. He didn't fancy weaving his way through the labyrinthine streets of South Canberra. They were rumoured to have been designed by a madman. The whole area was now a jumble of ramshackle dwellings, chook pens and vegetable gardens. The nearby suburb of Yarralumla, once renowned for its embassies, was now so taken up with horticultural produce as to be renamed Marrowlumla.

Crispin decided to manoeuvre his way through the labyrinth on his other means of transport, the Presidential bicycle. He rode with as much decorum as the dirt tracks that meandered through the district would allow.

The Nabob of Narrabundah was having tea with the Marchioness of Manuka when Crispin arrived.

'Greetings, Mr President,' said the Nabob. 'Welcome to my humble establishment.'

As establishments go, it was indeed humble: it consisted of a single brick structure which, if decrepit, was definitely an improvement on the shanties of his peasants. They were cobbled together (the shanties that is, not the peasants) out of bits and pieces of anything that looked like they could serve as a roof, door or wall.

'Tea, Mr President?' offered the Marchioness. The tea, like the shanties, was also cobbled together, in this case from a mixture of herbs, since Indian and Chinese blends of the beverage had long been unavailable.

'What news from the Capitol?' asked the Nabob while Crispin was sipping his tea. Crispin explained to him about the need to resume mining.

The Nabob didn't seem interested. 'Any news about the war?'

'The war is over. The Baron von Belco has been deposed and exiled. The Caliph of Kalang and the Archon of Aranda have made peace with the North Canberrans. The Baron's Beastly Boys have been gainfully employed, pulling down the GDE.'

'I meant the other war.'

'What other war?'

The Nabob and the Marchioness looked at each other in alarm. 'Haven't you heard? The people of Weston Creek have rebelled against the Warlord of Woden.'

15. The Laird of Lyons

Her name was Priscilla Hogg and she was a portly, pretentious, pompous person. In deference to ancient legend, people called her Miss Piggy. She was the Chairman of Chapman. Strictly speaking, she should have been Chairwoman, or perhaps Chairperson, but in the long run, linguistic fluency will always win out over ideological correctness.

It is said that the reason she advocated that Weston Creek should break away from the Warlord of Woden's control is because he had knocked back her advances. He may have feared that she was trying to gain some political hold over him, whereas her intentions were purely lustful: he was tall, noble and manly and she fancied him.

The Warlord was a polite, if ruthless man. He was too couth to tell her that he wasn't that desperate, especially given the number of winsome wenches in his domain.

Priscilla gathered together her colleagues, including the Reve of Rivett, the Duke of Duffy and the Webmaster of Weston Creek to discuss the situation. They all thought that Weston

Creek had its own specific identity, and surely no-one would object if they broke away from Woden.

She had also invited Melissa, the Fisher King (another gender misnomer), who had declined to attend.

'It's all right for you,' Melissa had complained, 'but we're right on the border with Woden.'

'We are erecting palisades on the Parkway at Hindmarsh Drive,' replied Priscilla. 'They should protect you.'

'The Warlord will find a way around them, I'm sure.'

***

He was tall, fair-haired, with a sporty moustache and a devil-may-care attitude. In days of yore, he was the sort that would have pranced around in front of the cameras, wearing a suit of Lincolnshire Green or a pirate's costume. His name was Igor Sputnik and he was the Laird of Lyons.

He used to speak in a phoney Russian accent – no-one in that part of the world having heard a genuine one for centuries – until he set his cap for the previous Laird's daughter. Bonnie Aimee McPherson said she'd nae marry him unless he became a Scotsman. This meant switching to a phoney Scots brogue.

One day, the Warlord of Woden called a meeting of his lieutenants to discuss the threat by Weston Creek to secede. He was waiting impatiently with two of his henchmen, the Prefect of Pearce and the Pharaoh of Phillip when Igor turned up with a miserable looking man of the cloth in tow – the Curate of Curtin.

'Where did you find him?' asked the Warlord.

'Hiding in a chicken coop,' Igor replied.

'Looking for the curate's egg, were we?' asked the Warlord, sarcastically.

'It's all right for you,' the Curate complained. 'But we're on the border with Weston Creek.'

'The Weston Creekers have erected palisades on the Parkway,' replied the Warlord. 'They should protect you until we pull them down.'

'Besides,' said Igor in his thick brogue, 'We're a lot closer to them than ye are, and we're not affeered.'

The Curate swallowed, and tugged awkwardly at his collar. 'Well, um, truth to tell, we're not very warlike in Curtin.'

When the other lords laughed at this comment, the Curate stumbled. 'In fact, we, uh, well …'

'Get on with it man,' snapped the Warlord.

'We're not happy about being part of Woden.' The Curate looked down, shame-faced.

'Not happy about being part of Woden,' the Warlord echoed slowly while drumming his fingers on the table.

'Er, yes, no, erm, what I mean is, with Curtin being named after a prime minister and everything, we feel we should be part of South Canberra.'

'Lyons is also named after a prime minister,' retorted the Laird, 'but we're nae joining that rabble.'

'Curtin may be named after a prime minister,' acknowledged the Warlord. 'But Woden is named after a god.'

***

The Parkway had once been a magnificent highway that stretched from Belcoway through the incomprehensible maze of Glenloch, and from there right down to Tuggeranong. Centuries of disuse and neglect had seen it crumble away into an embankment, similar to the GDE on the northern side.

The Warlord lined some of his troops on the eastern side of the palisades at Hindmarsh Drive, while Priscilla and her lieutenants lined theirs up on the Weston side.

'Little pig, little pig,' demanded the Warlord. 'Let me come in.'

***

It was all a diversion. The Laird of Lyons took his troops to cross the embankment further south, to attack Fisher from below, so to speak. The Fisher residents, having anticipated this move, had responded by putting up a sign:

The Laird took no notice of this. He snuck into the kitchen of Melissa's house, where she was preparing sandwiches for the troops, put his arms around her, and shouted 'Boo!'

Melissa giggled. 'Igor, you wicked fellow. What would Aimee say?'

'Da. Is all right. She does na' have to know.'

'And what are you doing here, you naughty boy?'

'We've coming to rape, loot, pillage and plunder, but maybe not in that order.'

'Oh. Well, I'm afraid you've caught us all unprepared. Is surrender an option?'

'Da. I suppose it is, lass,' replied the Laird with a touch of disappointment in his voice. 'Och! You're not much fun, are ye?'

Melissa smiled. 'That depends on your definition of fun.'

***

In due course, the Laird and his layabouts marched up Baddie Street, whence they encountered a formidable sight. Confronting them was the Wizard of Waramanga, in full regalia. He began waving his arms about and chanting weird cries. They had no idea what he was saying and neither did he.

Igor walked up to him, shoved his pointy wizard's hat down over his head and spun him around three times. The Wizard fell in a heap and the layabouts marched onwards to the palisades on Hindmarsh Drive.

'Not by the hairs of my chinny-chin-chin,' replied Priscilla.

'So. You have hairs on your chin, do you?' retorted the Warlord. Even Priscilla's supporters gathered on the Weston side of the palisades found this amusing.

'What are you going to do, eh?' demanded Priscilla. 'Huff and puff and blow the palisades down?'

The response came, not from the other side, but immediately to the defenders' right. The Laird and his layabouts had crept up on them. They chanted, 'Prissie's a pi-ig, Prissie's a pi-ig.'

The Weston Creekers drew back in alarm, except from Priscilla. 'Cowards,' she cried. 'We outnumber them.' She picked up a stick, snorted and charged at the Lyons layabouts.

She was not related to the Baron von Belco, but he would have been proud of the way she wielded her stick, striking snout and crown and sending the invaders reeling. Inspired, her comrades joined in, giving the invaders what for and driving them back. On the other side of the embankment, the Warlord and his troops were impotent.

'There were too many of them,' complained the Laird of Lyons while nursing a bloody nose, back at Melissa's house.

'I did warn you. Don't mess with Priscilla Hogg.'

'Aye. She's a demon.' Igor smiled. 'I wonder what she'd be like in knee length boots and a wee leather kilt?'

Melissa smiled. 'Do you really want to know?'

***

'My apologies,' replied the Warlord. 'But you moved into position rather more quickly than I expected. Did the people of Fisher offer no resistance at all?'

'Nyet. They are all pacifists.'

'Then we will have to try some other way.'

'Is it worth the effort?' asked the Laird, as he felt the throbbing in his nose. 'As long as the Parkway palisades exist, there will always be a barrier between us.'

'Hmm. It seems that they cannot be removed easily. You were able to penetrate from the south, where I'm sure they will strengthen their defences. Perhaps if we also tried from further north.'

'In that case, there might be a way.'

***

It was several days later when the Laird and his layabouts crept along Devonport Street, then across bare, hilly ground until they reached the point where it dipped down to go underneath the Parkway, to link Lyons with Weston Creek. That was long, long ago, but there was still a wee tunnel through the collapsed remains, if one knew where to look for it.

Igor had asked the Curate to join them, but he said that as a man of the cloth, it wasn't appropriate that he take part in tribal warfare. Besides, he hinted mysteriously that he had 'other fish to fry'.

The Laird and his gallant band worked their way through the tunnel to the far side, then started to creep into Weston Creek. They didn't get very far. A band of defenders was waiting for them.

'Going somewhere, boys.' Priscilla Hogg was standing there, wearing knee-length boots and a leather kilt, and wielding a large stick.

Realising that he had been betrayed, Igor uttered a blood-curdling cry and rushed straight at her. She uttered a similar cry and rushed straight at him. Meantime, the other would-be invaders turned and ran, scrambling as fast as they could back into the tunnel. The Weston Creekers followed them part of the way, then turned back. When they returned, Priscilla was wrestling on the ground with Igor. She snarled at her followers to go away.

***

Later that night, feeling pleased with himself, Igor sauntered back to his home. He wasn't sure whether he had dissuaded Priscilla from seceding from Woden and he didn't much care.

The light was still on in his bedroom, even though he had told Aimee not to wait up for him. Seeing a still form beneath the bedclothes, he plonked down on the edge of the bed and pulled off his boots. He was about to get into bed when Aimee walked into the bedroom.

She was startled and so was he.

'Then who—?' Igor pulled back the bedclothes. 'Curate, what are you doing here?'

16. Blasphemy

In an age when electronic media had long since ceased, and transport was by bicycle, horse, or on foot, one would expect news to travel slowly. By some mysterious means, rumour, gossip and scandal spread rapidly, in defiance of the lack of mass communications and rapid transport.

Most people had long known of the philandering ways of Igor Sputnik, Laird of Lyons – everyone, presumably, except his wife, the bonnie Aimee McPherson. It was therefore a big shock when word got out, as it inevitably would, that Igor came home to find her in bed with the Curate of Curtin.

Whether she really fancied the Curate, who was not the most handsome of men, or whether she was just getting her own back on her errant husband, Aimee caused a stir. Most people took the view that it served Igor right, and that he'd got his comeuppance at last.

The significance of the incident was not lost on the Warlord of Woden and his two main lieutenants.

The Prefect of Pearce stroked his bushy moustache thoughtfully. 'So all this talk about Curtin seceding from the Woden Union was just a ruse?'

'Evidently,' replied the Warlord. 'The Curate feigned indifference to the Union while all the time lusting after Mistress McPherson.'

The Pharaoh of Phillip adjusted his blue and gold striped headpiece while he conjured up an image in his mind of a petite lassie with red hair and ample bosoms. When she wore one of her short kilts … 'Every man in Woden lusts after the Lady of Lyons.'

'Quite so,' the Warlord agreed. He also conjured up similar images in his mind. 'Igor has reportedly defected to Weston Creek.'

'Is he going to join up with Chairman Priscilla?' asked the Prefect. The three men laughed at the thought of the lecherous Igor plighting his troth with the porcine lady.

'Somehow,' replied the Warlord. 'I think he might have other fish to fry.'

***

Melissa the Fisher King giggled. 'Igor, darling, I wish you wouldn't fondle me while I'm making sandwiches.'

'You are always making sandwiches,' he complained.

'I do run a catering business,' she reminded him.

Igor was surprised. 'You run a business?' Private businesses were a rarity in a society that had largely reverted to a pre-industrial co-operative economic system.

'Our family has been in catering since … way back when. There are lots of hungry workers out there in the fields that need nourishment, and sandwiches are a convenient way of providing it.'

'How do they pay for it?'

'They give bags of wheat to the miller, who passes on flour to the baker, who supplies me with the bread. Or they may pay me directly with vegetables, eggs and chicken meat that I put into their sandwiches.'

Igor straightened his kilt. 'Is this capitalism?'

Melissa pulled a face. 'Well, not really. After all, you can't have capitalism with capital, and hardly anyone has any capital to invest in anything. So there's none invested in the business. I just make sandwiches and trade them for the things I need to make more sandwiches. What goes around, comes around.'

Igor twirled around slowly. 'What goes around comes around.'

'I think that's true in love as well,' she added, pointedly.

Igor nodded. The thought occurred to him that he always got a good feed at her place. He remembered the hungry days of his youth, when there were a series of harvest failures. 'Can you be sure of always getting enough food?'

'These days, I usually can. Things do seem to be getting better, bit by bit.'

***

'Bit by bit, things are getting better,' echoed Norman. 'In the last half-century, mean temperatures have dropped by half a degree, and CO_2 levels have fallen below 350 parts per million. A few more decades, and they may be back to where they were at the start of the Industrial Revolution.'

'Will temperatures go back to what they were at that time?' asked Maya.

'No. That will take longer, because of the heat already in the atmosphere and the oceans. But the climate should be noticeably cooler and rainfall more regular.'

'And food production will increase?'

'Yes. People will get more to eat, which means they should live longer. Can you imagine? Before Gaia's Curse, people were actually worried about being too fat.'

'They didn't know when they were well off,' mused Maya.

'And we'll be better off. Siro and Anu, I mean. More to eat means more education. If only we had more metal.'

'Why?'

Norman looked up at the small radio transmission mast that Siro maintained on Black Mountain. 'To make more crystal sets. Think of how many people we could educate if we had thousands of sets instead of the few dozen we have scattered around town.' He added ruefully, 'I think the big cities have largely been mined out. It means we'll have to dig it out of the ground again. And,' he added hesitantly, 'smelt it.'

'What does that mean?'

'Extract it from the rock. Remove the impurities. But that means using coke.'

'What's that?'

He leant over and whispered in her ear. Maya was aghast. He had used another four-letter 'c' word. A word that dared not be uttered in the age of global warming.

'But that's blasphemy,' she breathed.

***

President Crispin VII also thought the idea was blasphemous. On the other hand, he realised that they did need more metal. When Norman paid him a visit, he set the President thinking.

'I don't suppose there is any other way we could smelt metals without using, er, coke.'

'It's needed for the manufacture of iron and steel,' explained Norman. 'Until we get some, we could try using char, which means burning wood. It still means producing lots of carbon dioxide.'

'Wasn't that the cause of Gaia's Curse?'

'It was. But that was by the human race producing over thirty billion tons of extra CO_2 per year. The amount that we'd produce would be miniscule.'

'We are still looking for mining sites where we can get metal,' replied the President. 'Where would we get this coke from?'

'There may be some places west of the mountains where we can get some. Otherwise, we are looking at sites north and south of Sydney.' Norman paused. 'It is possible that other regions have already starting producing metals again.'

'Then could we not buy the metals from them?'

'We could. Assuming that we have anything to sell that they would wish to buy.' Norman paused again. 'Of course, whichever region did start producing metal would have a tremendous advantage.'

'In what way?'

'For a start, they could make more solar panels and generate more power. They could then manufacture electric vehicles to transport people and goods.' For a third time, he paused. 'They could also forge weapons. If they don't gain dominance through economic power, they could do it through military might. They would become the most powerful region in Australia. In time, they would unite and rule the country.'

Crispin gave Norman a dark look. 'What you're saying is, if we are not the first to make metals, then some other region will become the ruler of Australia?'

'Precisely.'

Crispin leant back in his chair. 'Do you know how Canberra came into being?'

'Erm, something to do with the old states, I think.'

'More particularly, the rivalry between Melbourne and Sydney. Canberra was set up to ensure that neither city, nor any state, could dominate the national agenda. It was the ultimate compromise.'

'So?'

'If one region industrialised, it is likely that others would in turn do so, independently of the first region. Supposing the rivalry between Melbourne and Sydney, or between other regions, was resumed?'

'Then it might become necessary for Canberra to again be the national capital as a political compromise?'

It was the President's turn to say, 'Precisely. As it was in the past, so it will be in the future. Canberra will be all things to all people.'

***

As he made his way back through the treacherous swamps of Burley Griffin, Norman pondered what the President had told him. Should Canberra be a passive player, then? Waiting for other regions to emerge as economic powers before it reasserted its position as national capital?

That was not good enough for Norman. From the time of the first European settlement, it had taken over a century before the national capital was created. Would it take another century for Canberra to reassert its prominence in Australia?

He wanted Canberra to take the initiative – to lead, to unite and to rule. And he wanted it to happen in his lifetime.

***

The next time the Warlord of Woden assembled his council, there was a new member. Aimee McPherson had divorced Igor, who was now 'shacked up' with the Fisher King, Melissa. Aimee had assumed the title of Lady of Lyons.

During the meeting, the Warlord noticed that she seemed to be giving him her undivided attention, and scarcely glanced at the Curate of Curtin. Was their affair just a passing fling?

The council reluctantly concluded that if Weston Creek wanted to become a separate region, the matter should be referred to President Crispin for arbitration.

After the meeting, Aimee hung back. It was evident that she wanted words with the Warlord.

17. A Taste of Coq au Vin

Helen Hart, Premier of the Supreme Council of the Tuggeranong Soviet sat in her office in what had once been a business park in Greenway. On the wall behind her, in between the portraits of Marx and Lenin, was her own likeness. Her portrait showed her dressed in council robes, with a steely expression, and thick eyebrows that made make her look too domineering for Helen's tastes.

She knew that she wasn't always popular, and was sometimes known as 'Helen Hartless'. Years ago, the Soviet had been a rabble, endlessly debating obscure points of procedure instead of getting on with the job of running Tuggeranong. The districts south of the Woodcock-Johnson Line – Conder, Banks, Gordon, Calwell and Theodore – had broken away from the Soviet, only to come under the control of the Count of Condor and his lieutenants.

The confusing situation could be likened to the chaos that Lenin had found when he returned to Russia during the First World War. He had organised a 'ginger group', the Bolsheviks, to take control of the Communist Party and ultimately the country. Drawing their inspiration from Lenin, a faction known as the Greenway Group had taken over the Supreme Council of the Tuggeranong Soviet, and Helen had been a prominent member of that group.

She'd had to make some hard decisions, but she'd drawn inspiration from her heroine of ages past, Julia the Redhead. In her day, Julia had made some difficult decisions, including passing the controversial Carbon Tax.

How big an effect the tax and subsequent schemes had on reducing greenhouse gas emissions was hard to say: Global Warming was not quite as bad as predicted, with temperatures rising by two degrees during the 21st century. This took the Earth right to the edge of what climate scientists regarded as the critical level.

Whether this was due to the three-quarter-hearted efforts of governments to reduce emissions, or whether it was never going to be quite as bad as predicted, no-one would ever know. It had still been pretty bad.

Helen was looking out over an expanse of space that often served as a market place. There had once been a large shopping emporium there, a Hyperdome, which had long since crumbled into ruins. The rubble had been cleared away, but in deference to its former name, people now called it Hyperspace.

At the moment, there were no stalls, and the area was serving as a parade ground. Sergeant Shilling was training the Elite Guard of the TPLA – the Tuggeranong People's Liberation Army.

They looked resplendent in their bright red uniforms, which was actually a problem. During the last raid by the chicken rustlers of the Cooma Confederacy, the Elite Guard had been reluctant to take them on in battle because they would have got their uniforms dirty. As highly trained fighting forces go, they made an excellent marching team.

How had the chicken rustlers penetrated so far into Tuggeranong, even to Kambah itself? They had marched, in narrow daylight (it was very cloudy at the time), up what had once been known as Drakeford Drive. Now, given Tuggeranong's penchant for poultry, it was known as Drake Drive.

Had the perfidious Count of Condor allowed them through the Woodcock-Johnson Line? Helen suspected she knew the answer to that question, and was planning her next move when she had a visitor. 'Ah, Comrade Sputnik. Welcome to the People's Soviet Republic of Tuggeranong.'

***

For his part, the Count of Condor was twirling his moustache while looking out to the terraced farmlands of the valley, where his peasants were toiling in the fields. This was as it should be. The Count was an aristocrat, descended from no less illustrious a lineage as the *Comptes du Coq au Vin*.

There had been 37 such counts. The first had earned his counthood at Hastings: he impressed William of Normandy when with a single blow, he decapitated King Harold's third cousin twice removed (on his mother's side).

Eight centuries later, the 37th Count had made the perfectly reasonable suggestion that all criminals, vagrants and other ne'er-do-wells should be executed so they could be fed to the starving poor of Paris. He was decapitated by Madame Guillotine during the French Revolution. The poor may have eaten him even if they couldn't stomach his opinions.

But the Count of Condor was a worried man. The chicken rustlers of Cooma could strike again at any time. Last time, he'd bought them off by allowing them through the Woodcock-Johnson Line on to Drake Drive. He was reluctant to let them through, but as extortionists go, they were very persuasive. The Line was built to stop his serfs seeking political asylum in the Soviet, where the standard of living was reputed to be higher.

What puzzled him was why, having captured so many chickens, the raiders needed any more. Surely they could breed up numbers with the ones they already had? He had thought of appealing to the Tuggeranong Soviet for help, but that would ultimately have meant loss of control of his little empire. He would have to look for allies elsewhere. The Warlord of Woden, perhaps? But could he be trusted?

'Trust no-one.' That was what his father had told him, and so far, he had followed his father's advice. But it had come at the cost of leaving himself seriously exposed to threats from south and north. Of his lieutenants, he could trust the Thane of Theodore and the Bailiff of Banks, but the Grand Master of Gordon and the Canon of Calwell were too close to the Line for comfort.

An alliance with the Baron von Belco had been a possibility, especially since they both believed in the feudal system. But now, the Baron had been discredited and had run away to the Brindabellas. Another possibility was to support the Karabar Khan is his bid to oust the Queen of Queanbeyan, but the outcome would still be uncertain, even with his support.

There was the President, but would Crispin support him? Probably not. That left only the Soviet itself. Should he try to wrest some of its thirteen districts away from it? That would also be difficult, given the control that Premier Hart exercised over her comrades.

So, in their respective offices, the Premier and the Count plotted and planned, and waited for future developments.

***

Helen spread a rumour. At Hastings, the Count's ancestor had not been a warrior, but part of the catering corps. With a single blow of his cleaver, he had decapitated Harold's cousin's chicken. It had run around until it jumped into a barrel of wine, and marinated itself. The resulting delicacy had so impressed William that he had made the fellow his official Counter of the Royal Chickens. The 37th chicken counter had saved his own head because, after the execution of King Louis and Marie Antoinette, he had used the guillotine to behead the royal chickens, and gave them to the poor.

The rumour may have been completely scurrilous, but Helen had few qualms about spreading it, since she doubted whether there ever was a Compte du Coq au Vin.

It wasn't long before the rumour spread south of the Woodcock-Johnson Line. The Canon of Calwell heard it when he went to visit his old friend, the Grand Master of Gordon one afternoon.

Being loyal to his clan, the Grand Master wore a kilt and sporran. So did the young man who was his guest, who told them the tale of the chicken counters. He didn't tell them that Helen Hart had given him the choice of attending a re-education camp or going south to spread the rumour.

'He's my nephew by marriage,' explained the Grand Master. 'Or at least, he was.'

'Weren't you the Laird of Lyons?' asked the Canon.

'Aye. That I was,' replied Igor Sputnik. 'Until Aimee gave me my freedom.'

The other two had a quiet chuckle. 'That's one way of putting it,' said the Grand Master.

'And Melissa? Has she given you your freedom as well?' asked the Canon.

'She has, how you say? Terminated my employment. I was her sandwich delivery man, but there are so many lonely ladies in Weston.'

'Including, I believe, the Chairman of Chapman,' added the Grand Master.

Igor cleared his throat. 'She, er, mistook my natural friendliness for amorous intentions.'

'Hell hath no fury like Priscilla scorned,' intoned the Canon.

'She has put a price on his head,' explained the Grand Master. 'So he has come here seeking political asylum.'

***

The Count of Condor fingered his moustache while listening to Igor's tale of woe.

'Why did you come to me instead of seeking asylum in the Tuggeranong Soviet?' the Count asked.

Igor looked shifty eyed as he thought of an answer. 'I've had enough of bossy women.'

The Count laughed. 'Do you know Helen Hart?'

'I met her once. Long ago.'

'Not so long ago,' said the Count. 'You met her last week. She doubtless persuaded you to spread the pernicious rumour about my ancestors. I have my spies, as you are hers.'

Igor's startled look showed that he had been found out. 'Really, Count. I must protest.'

The Count took a large sword from the scabbard mounted on wall behind him. He swished it back and forth. 'The penalty for espionage against my person is instant death.'

Igor went down on his knees. 'Mercy, Count, mercy.'

'Not a very brave fellow, are you? Which is unfortunate, because I will spare your miserable life if you go on a little errand for me.'

'Anything, Count. Anything.'

'I want you to go to the Cooma Confederacy. Incognito, if that is possible in your case. Use your fatal charm if you have to, but I want you to find out why the Confederacy is stealing so many chickens.'

18. The Cooma Confederacy

'Sergeant Shilling?'

The sergeant approached Helen Hart, Premier of the Supreme Council of the Tuggeranong Soviet and gave a neat salute. 'Yes, ma'am?'

'Your troops are very well drilled.'

'Thank you, ma'am.' He looked with pride at the smartly turned out men and women on the Greenway parade ground.

Premier Hart put a matronly arm round his shoulder as they walked. 'Yet it occurs to me that if your troops can be trained in parade ground manoeuvres, then they can be trained in other things.'

Shilling eyed her warily. 'Such as?'

'The function of soldiers is to fight, is it not?'

'Well, to defend, and to give the people a sense of security.'

'Yet the one time they were called on to defend, as you put it, they failed miserably.'

The sergeant winced. He remembered when a raucous band of chicken rustlers had swept into Tuggeranong and taken away cartloads of poultry. His soldiers were singularly inept at dealing with the desperados.

'They, er, didn't want to get their uniforms dirty, ma'am. It would give a bad impression, and that would erode the confidence of the people.'

'Don't you think that failing to stop the chicken rustlers would erode their confidence even more?'

'Er, well …'

'If your troops can be well-trained to march, they can be well-trained in the arts of war.'

'But that would mean getting their uniforms dirty.'

'Their uniforms will be confiscated until they prove their worth in battle. If they win, they can wear their fancy costumes at their victory parade. There will be war soon, and I want them to be ready for it.'

Sergeant Shilling realised his job could be on the line. 'I will train them to defend Tuggeranong to the last man or woman.'

'I didn't say anything about defending, Sergeant. I said there would be war soon, and so there will be.'

***

The King of the Cooma Confederacy was a swarthy, weather-beaten man who looked like he had seen many summers and many fights – his appearance was ferocious. This was deliberate; technically, he was the president of a federation of alpine states. Over the centuries, his position had become hereditary, and had become known as the King. But his grip on power, amidst the scattered and often fractious clans of his domain was tenuous, and so he had to emphasise what power he had.

Certainly, the miserable wretch who grovelled before him seemed impressed. The King sat upon a large, stiff-backed chair on a dais.

'Who are you?' demanded the King.

'M-my name is Igor Sputnik, and I come to claim political asylum.'

'Asylum? From whom?'

'I-I was a slave of the Count of Condor, but I escaped from his cruel service.'

'Then is there any reason why I should not send you back to him?'

The wretch quivered, then a sly look came over his face. 'I could help you find the best poultry farms to raid.'

'Indeed? And why should I want to raid poultry farms?'

Igor looked surprised. 'You are always attacking his.'

'That's news to me. Of course, I cannot be held responsible for what some of my subjects might be getting up to.' The King looked at the burley guard who was towering over Igor. 'Corporal Grunt, where did you find this miserable wretch?'

'He was skulking around the chicken coup, sire.'

'So. Planning a little raid of your own, were you? Very well. Set him to work mucking out the chook yard.'

As Corporal Grunt led Igor away, a young woman entered the room. She was slender, with raven tresses and a comely face. She looked at Igor, who winked at her.

'Father, who is that strange man?'

'Mm?' The king was distracted. 'He is a spy, sent by the Count of Condor to find out who is organising the chicken raids on his domains. That wretch's name is Igor Sputnik. Now, where have I heard that name before?'

'Why is he wearing a dress?'

'That's not a dress, my dear. It's a kilt. He's a Scotsman … Of course. The Laird of Lyons. He is reputed to have a roving eye.' The King turned sharply towards his daughter. 'Isobel, he is a very dangerous man. No woman is safe with him around. I forbid you to go anywhere near him.'

***

Poor Igor. He hadn't known when he was well off. He'd had a cushy job when he was Laird of Lyons. Things had gone from bad to worse since Aimee had thrown him out for fooling around with Melissa the Fisher King. Melissa had thrown him out for offering the comely housewives of the Weston Union more than just sandwiches. Priscilla Hogg, the Chairman of Chapman, had wanted him all to herself. And then there was Helen Hart, Premier of the Tuggeranong Soviet.

Now, here he was, forced to do manual work for a living, and mucky work at that. But, truth to tell, he had been bored with Aimee. He needed new adventures, and close encounters of the amorous kind.

He envied the rooster as it strutted around the yard. Perhaps Igor should have got himself a harem. The Wazir of Watson had four wives. But having wives meant having responsibilities, especially if they had any children. Not the life for a free spirit like Igor.

Then, there was the lassie he had just seen in the court of the King of Cooma. Now there was a worthy challenge.

'Hsst.'

Igor looked up. To his great joy, the young lady in question was standing just outside the chicken coop, glancing furtively around her.

'Aye, lassie. What can I do for 'e?'

'Are you really a wicked Scotsman?' she asked, wide-eyed.

'Well, I am a Scotsman,' he lied. 'As for the wicked bit, that's for me to know and ye to find out.' He winked at her again.

'There's a question I've always wanted to ask a Scotsman.'

***

Three months later, a bedraggled figure arrived at the court of the Count of Condor. He looked as though he had been hiding out in bushland, and living off the land as best he could. He would glance nervously over his shoulder, as if he was expecting pursuers.

'Well, well, well. Master Sputnik, is it not?'

'Aye, milord.'

'Did I not send you to the King of Cooma to find out why he is stealing our chickens?'

'You did, milord. But the King and his minions have not been doing the rustling.'

'Indeed. Who is it, then?'

'A group called the Brindabella Brigands. They are said to be the feral descendants of the rangers of the Namadji Park. Recently, they started to raid the King's domains as well.'

The Count stroked his thin moustache. 'Did they indeed? The Brindabella Brigands, eh? Then it seems that the King of Cooma and I have common cause.'

'I-I would na' trust him that far.'

'So tell me, how did you escape?'

'Escape?'

'Last I heard, the King suspected you of being a spy, and had you cleaning out his chicken coop.'

'How did you know that?'

A burly fellow walked into the room. 'Because I told him.'

Igor's heart sank. It was Corporal Grunt. He quickly realised the truth. 'I've been set up.'

'He escaped with the brigands when they raided the king's chickens,' explained the corporal. 'Now the king wants him, and his chickens, back.'

'I can oblige the king with his first request,' said the Count. 'Ask him to please accept the former Laird of Lyons as a peace offering.'

'No, Count,' protested Igor. 'Have mercy. The King will torture me.'

'He will indeed. A torture known as marriage. Something about his daughter being in the family way, I believe.'

'She-she canna marry me. I'm already married to Aimee McPherson.'

'Mistress McPherson divorced you, and has married the Warlord of Woden.' Seeing Igor's jaw drop, the Count added, 'look on the bright side. Isobel is the King's only child. Marry her, and you will be heir to his throne. No more mucking out the chicken coop. And perhaps you could exercise your royal prerogative with the ladies of Cooma.'

Igor's eyes brightened. 'I had na' thought of that.'

Corporal Grunt reached forward to grab him. 'Come along, you.'

'Get your hands off me, varlet. You will show the heir to the throne proper deference.' Igor swirled his cape round his shoulders. 'Come, let us away.'

Corporal Grunt bowed. 'Yes, Prince Igor.'

'Prince Igor? Da. Is good. I like that.'

They were about to leave when a flunky burst into the room. 'Count, Count. The peasants are revolting.'

'Nyes, aren't they?' The Count preened himself.

'No, Count. They are in revolt. They are helping the Tuggeranong People's Liberation Army to tear down the fence, and are fleeing through the gaps to Tuggeranong.'

'What!' roared the Count. 'Call out the guard!'

Soon, the Count's domain was a hive of activity. Soldiers were running around with staves, while the Count, having mounted his trusty steed, was galloping off madly in all directions at once, shouting orders at everybody.

Igor and the corporal left amid the confusion. South was now a very desirable direction. It seemed that events were conspiring to push Igor into the loving arms of the comely Isobel. He remembered an old quotation: 'there's a divinity that shapes our ends, rough-hew them how we will.'

Corporal Grunt thought for a moment. 'Hamlet. Act Five. Scene Two ...'

19. The Brindabella Brigands

Even as Igor had been making his way back to the Count of Condor's domain, an incident took place elsewhere that would have a big bearing on events to come.

On the edge of the Brindabellas, three layabouts were lying about on the verge of what had once been a road, but was now just a glorified path. They were hoping to waylay the odd wayfarer that made the mistake of venturing into what they regarded as their domain.

Their leader, Doug, was a tall, dark haired man with a long nose that had been broken, giving him a fearsome appearance. In contrast, his offsiders were a pair of short, scruffy ruffians, or scruffians.

This day, they were in luck, or so they thought; they saw a traveller approaching. Although of robust build, he had a slight limp. He carried a haversack and was aided by a thick walking staff. His bullet-shaped head was bowed as he muttered to himself about useless ninnies and gutless wonders, and why was he always surrounded by idiots?

Doug stepped out in front of the traveller, while his scruffians moved to flank their intended victim.

'What have you got in that sack?' demanded Doug.

The traveller stopped. His ginger moustache bristled. 'What business is it of yours?'

'Listen. We are the Brindabella Brigands. Don't mess with us.'

'Brigands? Brindabella Bludgers, more like. Now let me pass.'

'Grab him lads.'

The lads moved in tentatively. There was something about this ginger-haired man that made them wary.

They were wise to be cautious. With a deft twirl of his staff, the traveller cracked Doug on the nose, breaking it in a second place. Then, with a quick back thrust, he jabbed the scruffian on his left in the solar plexus, leaving him gasping for air by the road side. The other turned and fled, helped on his way by a hefty whack on the derriere.

Doug was still holding his nose when the traveller came up to him. 'Don't mess with the Baron von Belco,' said the ginger-haired man, emphasising his words by jabbing Doug in the ribs with his staff.

Then the traveller went on his way, chanting, 'hit them with your rhythm stick.' There was now a spring in his step. Giving someone a damn good thrashing had worked like a tonic.

***

An hour later, Doug and his scruffians limped back to their camp. The sentry was rubbing his ribs. At the campfire, their Fearless Leader, Bald Eagle was holding a cloth to a nasty bruise on his bald pate. The Baron was sitting in Bald Eagle's chair, munching on a chicken bone.

'About time you layabouts got back here,' said the Baron. 'As you can see, I am now in command of this rabble. And rabble you are. Tomorrow, I shall start turning you into a proper fighting force.'

'To do what?' asked Doug.

'To do battle. To conquer. To rule. No more skulking about in the bushes or stealing chickens. We've got some real pillaging to do.'

***

Prince Igor and Corporal Grunt were just leaving the outskirts of Banks when they saw a pompous man with a ginger moustache and a bullet-shaped head leading a band of ne'er-do-wells marching abeam of them. They looked as professional as a band of scruffians could. They sang as they marched:

With hobnail boots, we trample on our foes
With hobnail boots, we stomp on all their toes.

In the distance could be heard other voices – the shouts and cries from the Battle of the Woodcock-Johnson Line.

'We're better off out of here,' suggested Corporal Grunt.

'Da. I do not think this will be a good day for the Count of Condor.'

***

The Battle of the Woodcock-Johnson Line is best described by onomatopoeia: bang, whack, thud, wallop, thump, stomp, ouch. The gallant heroes of the TPLA were trying to pull down sections of the fence that prevented the oppressed masses, held in feudal servitude by that perfidious reactionary, the Count of Condor from being embraced into the bosom of the Tuggeranong motherland. The Count's troops arrived to drive the heroes back. At first, they fought in a disciplined way with staves, but they soon resorted to fisticuffs.

All-in brawls ensued. They were complicated by some of the oppressed masses trying to fight their way through the gaps being torn in the fence, and getting caught up in the mêlées. In the confusion, sometimes they fought with the Count's men, and sometimes with their Tuggeranong liberators, who were not allowed to wear their uniforms.

Meanwhile, the Count was riding around from one trouble spot to another, brandishing his ceremonial sword while exhorting his troops and driving back his serfs. Then, one of his flunkeys brought him some disturbing news: 'Your Excellency.

It's the Brindabella Brigands. They're attacking Banks.' The Count snarled, and rode off to confront the villains.

The Baron von Belco was 'requisitioning poultry' when a man waving a sword rode up to him. Most men would have cowered in terror, but the Baron stood his ground.

'What are you doing here?' demanded the rider.

'Having a picnic,' retorted the Baron. His men laughed.

The rider bristled. 'You will leave immediately or I will have you all flogged.'

The Baron approached the rider. 'Flogged, eh? And who do you think you are?'

'I am the Count of Condor.'

'Is that so?' With a deft flick of his stick, the Baron knocked the sword out of the Count's hand. 'And I am the Baron von Belco. A Baron outranks a Count. So you will do as I say.' He nodded to his men, who rushed in and dragged the Count from his horse. He pushed the tip of his staff to the Count's throat. 'Your useless ninnies are no match for my men.'

'Maybe so,' sneered the Count. 'But they're busy fighting off the marauding hordes of the Tuggeranong army, who have attacked our perimeter in five places. If they break through and overrun my domain, neither of us will be giving orders to anybody.'

The Baron pulled out an old chart, a crude representation of the count's domain. 'Show me where.'

The Count marked five crosses on the Woodcock-Johnson Line.

'Very well,' said the Baron. 'Tell your men to hold their ground. We shall deal with the incursions, one by one. Provided you agree to my terms.'

'Which are?'

'You can remain as Count of Condor, but you will recognise me as your overlord.'

The Count sighed. He knew the situation was desperate. 'It seems I don't have much choice.'

***

Helen Hart, Premier of the Supreme Council of the Tuggeranong Soviet, had devised the attack plan. The TPLA was divided into five platoons, each about twenty strong. She had indicated the points along the Woodcock-Johnson dividing fence where they would launch their attacks. She wasn't sure how successful they would be, but even making one or two breaches in the fence would let many of the oppressed serfs through.

She was perturbed, late in the day, to see Sergeant Shilling hobbling back with a bloodstained bandage on his head. Helen feared the worst. 'What went wrong?'

'We were succeeding,' insisted the Sergeant. 'Until the Brindabella Brigands turned up and attacked our positions, one after the other. They formed themselves into small wedges and charged, whacking everyone in their path. We didn't stand a chance.' He managed a weak smile. 'At least, some of the serfs got through.'

'The Brindabella Brigands?' Helen frowned. 'That doesn't sound like their style.'

'They've got a new leader. A man with a ginger moustache and a bullet-shaped head. And they were singing some silly song about trampling on everyone.'

Helen thought for a moment. 'The Baron von Belco? He was overthrown and driven out of his territory.'

'Well, he's back now.'

'Indeed. That's bad news for us, but even worse news for the Count of Condor. The Baron has a simple philosophy: he is Number One, and everybody must obey him, or he will hit them.'

'What are we going to do?'

'Seek help from an old, er, acquaintance.'

***

The Warlord of Woden was surprised when he was told that Helen Hart wanted an audience. He thought back fondly to a warm, moonlit night when … Aimee entered the room. He snapped out of his reverie. 'We have a visitor, my dear,' he said as he motioned her to sit by his side.

Helen Hart entered cautiously. The sight of Aimee's bulging belly was enough to convince her that any renewal of a special relationship with the Warlord was probably out of the question.

The Warlord received her graciously. 'To what do we owe the honour of this visit, Madame Premier?'

'I have come to seek your assistance.' She outlined what had happened, before adding, 'I'm sure the Baron will not be content with control of the Count of Condor's domains. In due course, he will attempt to take over the whole of Tuggeranong. After that, who knows?'

Aimee looked worried. 'You mean, he might attack us?'

Helen nodded. 'He is a megalomaniac.'

The Warlord steepled his hands for a moment, looked at Aimee, then at Helen. 'What would you have us do?'

'Can you send troops to help us?'

'Hmm. I'm not sure that our troops would be any better at fighting the Baron's than yours were.' He thought ruefully of their failed attempts to subdue the Weston Creekers. 'But there is somebody who might be able to help.'

'Who is that?'

'The only man ever known to have bettered the Baron in a fight. The Tyrant of Turner.'

20. The Battle of Greenway

Three hooded figures strode out of the north, and into the heart of Tuggeranong's Greenway district. The locals stared at them in wonder: they looked like the sort of people you wouldn't want to tangle with. Two of them carried quarter staves, while the third had an arrow and quivers.

Waiting to meet them were Helen Hart, Sergeant Shilling, and members of the TPLA, who were showing signs of wear and tear.

'Welcome, lady and gentlemen,' said Helen Hart.

The strangers pulled back their hoods. The two men looked similar – square-jawed and steely-eyed, except that one had streaks of grey in his beard while the other was young and clean-shaven. The audience gasped when the archer pulled back her hood to reveal a trim slip of a girl.

'I am Mordred Guard,' said the older man, 'Tyrant of Turner. This is my son Trex, Captain of the North Lyneham Guard and his fiancée Diana, huntress of O'Conner.'

'Can you rid us of this troublesome beast?' asked Helen.

'The Baron? Has he made any move against you yet?'

'Not directly. But he and his men often walk up and down Woodcock and Johnson Streets while singing rude songs.'

'He has made no effort to repair the damaged fences,' added Sergeant Shilling. 'Once, he stepped through onto our territory and blew a raspberry.'

'That sounds like the Baron,' muttered Trex.

'Hmm.' The Tyrant nodded. 'Unfortunately, when he gets word of our arrival, he may decide to strike before we can get your troops battle-ready.'

'How long will that take?' asked Sergeant Shilling.

'We'd best get started right away. Fortunately, I believe your troops are already good at drill work. Working from the known to the new, we must incorporate weapons training into your existing routines. But we're going to need more recruits. And a lot of quarter staves.'

***

The Warlord of Woden found himself making more visits to the capital than hitherto, to give frequent reports to President Crispin VII at the formerly splendid House On The Hill.

'What news from Tuggeranong?' asked the President, who had been the intermediary between the Warlord and the Tyrant of Turner.

'I gather that progress has been slow,' replied the Warlord. 'The valiant heroes of the TPLA are discomfited when they get their knuckles barked in quarter stave training. Also, they are upset by their new uniforms.'

'Why?'

'Instead of being bright red, they are a greenish-brown colour, which is better suited to combat duty.'

'Well, I daresay Premier Hart will exhort them to make sacrifices for the glorious motherland.'

At that point, a messenger entered and spoke briefly in hushed tones to the President, whose response was, 'why am I not surprised?'

'Is something wrong?' asked the Warlord.

'It seems that the Karabar Khan and the Begum of Jerra have moved against the Queen of Queanbeyan. I had been expecting this. The Queen has been showing symptoms of …'

'Senility?'

'Forgetfulness. Dear, oh dear. How it all changes.'

***

Jezebel, the Begum of Jerra had long since decided to emulate her namesake by being a femme fatale. With a dress slit up her thighs, her coquettish looks and beguiling voice, she had entranced Quentin, the Karabar Khan and drawn him into her web of intrigue.

'Quentin, darling,' she said to him one morning in her husky voice. 'It's time we made our move.'

The first the residents of Queanbeyan realised there was anything amiss was when the troops of the Khan and the Begum marched from the showgrounds to surround the former council offices that now served as the palace. 'Just a routine training exercise,' they told everyone.

Quentin and Jezebel went inside to see the Queen.

'Well, if it isn't Christopher Robin and Alice,' said Queen Doris, who was dusting the palace.

'My name is Quentin,' insisted the young Khan.

Jezebel viewed him askance. 'I believe it was a literary allusion.'

'She's the one under the illusion,' insisted Quentin. 'We've come to——'

'Take her out on a picnic,' said Jezebel, as she took the Queen by the arm.

'Well, that's very nice of you, dears,' said Her Majesty, with a twirl of her feather duster.

When they led her outside, she noticed the troops. 'A guard of honour. How nice.'

'Not exactly,' said Quentin, as some of his troops moved in front of and others behind the royal party. 'This is a cowp dettat.'

'A what?' asked the Queen. 'Oh. A *coup d'état*. Young man, if you're going to stage a coup, then at least you could learn to pronounce it properly.'

They put her on to a cart and led her away towards the river. 'Where are you taking me?'

'We're putting you out to pasture,' explained Jezebel. 'There's a nice retirement village upstream.'

'This is the duck farm,' said the Queen, when they arrived.

'Yeah,' said Quentin. 'You can spend the rest of your days feeding the ducks.'

The Queen looked at her captors doubtfully. Jezebel slipped her a wink. The Karabar Kid and his cronies were useful for doing the donkey work of staging a coup, but the Begum would soon manoeuver him out of the way.

***

Meanwhile, in Cooma, events were transpiring that would have no bearing on what was happening in Canberra, but fans of Igor Sputnik may be dying to know what happened to him.

'Prince Igor', as he now called himself, was married to Isobel, daughter of the King of Cooma. In due course, she was delivered of a baby boy. They had to think of a name for him.

'Hamish is such a nice Scottish name,' said Isobel, who preferred Igor when he was imitating a Scot rather than a Russian.

'I want to name him Vladimir,' insisted Igor. 'After our national hero, Putin the Great.'

The King of Cooma settled the issue. 'Alexander,' he said gruffly. 'It's a famous Russian and Scottish name.'

'Ah, like Alexander Nevski,' said Igor.

'Or Alexander Ogg,' added Isobel.

***

The Baron von Belco called together his lieutenants – the Count of Condor, the Bailiff of Banks, the Thane of Theodore, the Canon of Calwell and the Grand Master of Gordon.

'Gentlemen,' said the Baron. 'The time has come for action. This afternoon, you will assemble your troops near but out of sight of the five gaps in the fence. In the morning, as soon as it is light enough to see, you will overpower the Tuggeranong guards, assuming there are any on duty at that time, march through the gaps and head straight for Greenway.'

'And what will you be doing?' asked the Canon of Calwell.

The Baron eyed the Canon warily. He trusted neither him nor the Grand Master of Gordon. Although they had not openly defied him, their attitude to him and the Count of Condor seemed to smack of a lack of enthusiasm.

'I shall be there ahead of you,' was his cryptic reply.

Afterwards, the Canon had a quiet word with the Grand Master. 'I don't like the sounds of this. The Baron is insufferable now. What's he going to be like if he takes over the whole of Tuggeranong?'

The Grand Master thought for a moment. 'Forewarned is forearmed. There is more than one way to get from Gordon to Tuggeranong.'

***

The Baron had learned his lesson from the O'Connor ridge fiasco, when his two groups of troops had fought each other in the middle of the night. Later that afternoon, he took his Brindabella Brigands west to the banks of the Budgie River. From there, they marched northwards, until they were abeam of Greenway.

'What now?' asked Bald Eagle.

'For now, we wait. Until first light.'

***

At first light, the Baron and his men rose up, headed swiftly through the scrub, and crept into Greenway. The few guards on duty were quickly overpowered. They were the Premier's personal guards, not members of the TPLA. The Baron bailed up one individual and demanded to know where the soldiers were.

'They, er, went on a three-day personal discovery retreat.'

'Retreat sounds like the sort of thing they would do.' The Baron and his men laughed. They soon entered the Great Hall of the People, the Premier's office, and even her personal apartments.

Having risen early, Helen Hart was eating breakfast when a group of Brigands burst in.

'What is the meaning of this outrage?' she demanded.

'You're our prisoner,' insisted Bald Eagle. 'Right lads. Take her away and lock her up. Our master will interrogate her later.'

The Brigands may have hoped that a stint in the cells would calm Helen down. But she was still seething when she was taken to see the Baron an hour later.

The Baron paced back and forth while eyeing her off. 'Hmm,' he said, appreciatively. 'Nice broad child-bearing hips. It's time I found myself a Baroness and produced an heir.'

'How dare you!' Helen slapped his face.

'How dare you!' The Baron slapped her face.

Next thing, they were grappling with each other, in a rough-and-tumble in the spacious office of the Premier of the Tuggeranong Soviet. Helen put up a pretty good fight, but the Baron's greater strength won out. Both were panting heavily as he pinned her to the floor.

Helen was outraged and impressed. No man had ever stood up to her like that before, let alone wrestled her to the floor. Well, perhaps one man. But the Warlord of Woden was now married.

'What is your star sign?' she asked, breathlessly.

***

The Baron was a Hairy Nosed Wombat and Helen Hart was an Emu. Centuries earlier, in a burst of patriotic fervour, Australians had decided to do away with the traditional star signs. With some imaginative drawing of lines between the stars in the southern sky, they had invented constellations which, with a lot more imagination, could be seen to depict the Wombat, the Emu, and the Bandicoot etc. Thus was Austrology created.

Whenever he was asked what his star sign was, the Tyrant of Turner used to reply, 'Socrates the Sceptic.'

But where was the Tyrant? For that matter, where was the Tuggeranong People's Liberation Army? The Baron's five lordlings did as they were told, and led their troops through the gaps in the fence. There was no-one around to stop them. In fact, there was no-one around at all.

This worried the Count of Condor. Surely some people should have been up and about by then? As he led his soldiers up Drake Drive, he suspected that a thousand pairs of eyes were peering out at them from behind drawn curtains.

The Baron had barely finished grappling with Helen Hart when the Count's troops arrived at the parade ground in Greenway, closely followed by those from Banks and Theodore. The Calwell forces, and those from Gordon, arrived some little time later, even though they had the shortest distances to march.

'Excellent,' said the Baron, after he had dusted himself off and locked Helen away again. Along with his Brindabella Brigands, he had well over a hundred men assembled before him.

While the Baron was inspecting his troops, the Count of Condor was keening his ears. Everything was quiet: deathly quiet. Then, he heard it, faint at first, but getting louder. A song? It seemed to be coming from the north, from the direction of Kambah. As it grew louder, he recognised it: the International. The Count's aristocratic nostrils flared. How dare they? Mere upstart peasants!

The red pennants of the TPLA were visible long before the marchers came into view – not a few dozen troops, nor even a hundred, but several hundred revolutionary heroes, some dressed in uniforms and some in workaday clothes, all wearing red bandannas and carrying quarter staves.

The logical thing to do would be to retreat, but the Baron was made of sterner stuff. Either that, or he was a raving nutter. He ordered his troops to line up in six wedge formations of twenty or thirty each. Those wedges in turn formed a larger wedge, with the Count of Condor – foaming at the mouth – and his troops at the front. Two more wedges followed, and then the other three at the back, including the Brindabella Brigands.

Sergeant Shilling and his legions stopped, barely fifty paces from the invaders. 'By command of the Supreme Soviet of the People's Republic of Tuggeranong, I order you to lay down your arms and surrender.'

There was silence. For a moment. Then came the Baron's answer: 'Cheearge!'

Brandishing their staves, the invaders charged towards the defenders, who thrust their staves forward to form a line of pickets. The crazed Count of Condor whirled his great ceremonial sword and shattered Sergeant Shilling's staff. Sweeping the Sergeant aside with the flat of his sword, he started to slash at the staves around him.

The air rattled with the sound of stick on stick, of fist on jaw, with the cries of those who struck and those who were struck. Led by the enraged Count of Condor, the invaders drove a deep wedge into the ranks of the defenders.

But if you can keep your head while those around you are losing theirs … a meek, tame political scientist and Marxist-Leninist theoretician named Colin waited until the Count came within range, then hurled his staff like a spear into the solar plexus of the class enemy of the people.

As the Count doubled up in pain, Colin wrenched the sword from his grasp. His comrades rushed in, picked up the Count, carried him over to nearby Lake Tuggeranong, and tossed him in. Because of Climate Change, that once glorious body of water was now a glorified mud hole, in which an inglorious Count gasped and wallowed in the slime.

By then, the weight of numbers was telling against the five wedges that had hurled themselves at the defenders of the revolution. One by one, the other four lordlings were picked up and tossed into the mud, although the Grand Master of

Gordon and the Canon of Calwell were treated a little more gently than the others.

Five wedges? But what happened to the sixth? The Brindabella Brigands had lagged behind the other wedges, then withdrew altogether. Once the Baron saw which way the Battle of Greenway was going, he ordered his men to follow him back to the administrative complex.

'We still have our hostage,' he told Bald Eagle.

Blocking their way was a hooded man with a staff. 'Hello, Baron,' said the Tyrant of Turner. 'We meet again.'

21. Convocation

The Baron reacted immediately. He roared and charged at the Tyrant of Turner while wielding his stave. The Tyrant parried several blows, dodged a couple of thrusts, and then riposted with some blows of his own.

In their previous encounter, when the Baron had swung his stave out wide, the Tyrant had used a fencing manoeuver known as a 'beat attack'. A short, outward-swinging blow had knocked the staff from the Baron's hands.

Once again, the Baron swung his stave out wide, and the Tyrant struck at it. But the Baron slackened his grip, causing the stave to fly out of his hands without resistance. The Tyrant briefly overbalanced. The Baron lunged, and gave his opponent an upper cut to the jaw. As the Tyrant crumpled to the ground, the Baron retrieved his stave. He was about to continue his flight when another figure loomed before him.

'Going somewhere, Baron?' asked Trex Guard.

The two of them traded blows alongside the recumbent form of Trex's father. Around them, a group of TPLA patriots had emerged from the administration complex and were battling with the Brindabella Brigands. That would all end in tears for the Brigands. After Bald Eagle was whacked on the head again, and Doug got his nose broken for the third time, the Brigands yielded.

Actually, they didn't so much surrender; the fighting ceased while they watched Trex and the Baron trade blows – youth, strength, dexterity and guile versus middle-age, strength, dexterity and guile.

In their previous battle, fought on O'Connor Ridge on a moonlit night, Trex felt he had been getting the upper hand when he had tripped over a small bush. This time, he was again gaining the upper hand, when he stepped back to wind up for a mighty swing just as his father regained his senses and started hauling himself to his feet.

Trex fell over his father and the two of them went sprawling in the dust. The Baron moved in to give Trex an almighty whack. In their previous battle, he had been about to do so when he had felt a sharp pain in his right buttock, courtesy of an arrow from Diana.

This time, he was about to whack Trex when he felt a sharp pain in his left buttock. He looked round to see Diana reloading her bow. Letting out a mighty roar, he charged straight at her and knocked the bow out of her hands. As she turned to flee, he gave her a whack on the rump. Diana was astonished: no-one had smacked her since she was a little girl. She burst into tears.

Enraged, Trex hauled himself to his feet. Ignoring the groan from his father beneath him, he lunged at the Baron with a rugby tackle that sent them sprawling to the ground.

'Ow,' cried the Baron. 'Get this thing out of me.'

'Not until you give us the key to the cells,' Trex insisted as he sat on top of him.

A short time later, a hobbling Baron was escorted to the cells. Trex had held him down while his father and Diana had pulled out the arrow. Trex opened the cell.

'About time,' insisted Premier Helen Hart, who had been incarcerated therein. She looked at the Baron. 'Oh, the poor dear, what happened to him?'

They lay the Baron face down on a bunk while Helen ordered her minions to get some water and bandages.

'You're not going to help him?' asked Trex in surprise.

'I used to be a nurse,' she replied. 'Now, help me get his trousers off.'

***

Oh, what a sore and sorry sight they were. The Baron, now in the care and custody of Helen Hart, had a bandaged behind and wounded pride. Helen's pride had also been wounded, and her face was still sore from where he had slapped her.

The Count of Condor had bruised ribs and was covered in mud. His lordlings were also mud-splattered. Bald Eagle had a bandage round his head, and Doug had one on his nose. All of these gentlemen and the rest of the Brigands were incarcerated.

Sergeant Shilling had fractured ribs and concussion, while dozens of the combatants were nursing bumps and bruises and fractures.

On his previous battle with the Baron, the Tyrant had suffered a nasty bruise to his right shoulder. This time, he had one on his left shoulder, and well as a sore jaw. Diana had a sore behind, and Trex was feeling pleased with himself.

'Sorry we were late getting to the battle,' he explained to Helen Hart. 'The Grand Master of Gordon warned us about the Baron's plan to attack in five places and converge on Greenway. We let his troops through so we could ambush them here. But we didn't know about the plan to raid your complex at dawn.'

To his surprise, Helen Hart didn't seem to mind. She seemed more preoccupied with her prisoner.

***

'Hello, dearie,' said Deirdre the herbalist, cheerfully. 'Ooh, that's a nasty lump on your shoulder, and your jaw. It's either a case of the mumps or you've been fighting with the Baron again.'

'The latter,' said the Tyrant of Turner.

'Cecil, dear,' called Deidre. 'A poultice for the nice gentleman.'

'Yes, milady,' said Cecil Underling, who was happy to be her slave.

***

'Welcome back, dears,' said Mrs Tyrant as her husband, son and Diana arrived home. 'Had a nice war, did we?'

'We won,' said the Tyrant, tersely.

'It doesn't look as though you did. You will insist at playing toy soldiers, even at your age.'

'Thank you, dear. I really needed that.'

'Oh. There's a message for you. From the President, no less.'

The Tyrant read the message while Mrs Tyrant fussed over Trex and Diana.

'I've been summonsed,' said the Tyrant.

'Summonsed,' echoed Trex. 'Why? What have you done?'

'It's not what I've done. It's who I am. The President has called a meeting, or convocation, of the leaders of the eight districts of the Canberra Region.'

***

In many cultures, through time and space, storm clouds, thunder and lightning were regarded as ominous portents. Even in less superstitious times, they made people feel uncomfortable.

But for the people of southern Australia, in the age of Gaia's Curse, when droughts were the norm, storm clouds filled their hearts with glee, lightning lit up their souls, and thunder and rain on the roofs were music to their ears.

So the storm clouds gathering over Parliament House as the delegates assembled for the Convocation were seen as a good omen.

There were two delegates from each district: Governor Percival Gerontius and Cyril Suckling from Gungahlin, the Caliph of Kalang and the Archon of Aranda from Belconnen, the Tyrant of Turner and the Grand Duke of North Lyneham from North Canberra, the King of Kingston and the Nabob of Narrabundah from South Canberra, the Warlord of Woden and the Pharaoh of Phillip, Priscilla Hogg and Melissa the Fisher King from the Weston Union, Premier Helen Hart and the Grand Master of Gordon from the recently reunified Tuggeranong Soviet, and Jezebel, the newly crowned Queen of Queanbeyan with her consort, the Karabar Khan. Norman, the Grand Wizard of Siro and Maya, High Priestess of Anu were also present.

President Crispin VII sat in the Speaker's chair in the House of Representatives and addressed his delegates.

'Centuries ago, as Gaia began to wreak her revenge upon the Earth, my ancestor President Crispin Spalding, saw his world disintegrate into nation states, which broke up into provinces and regions, and they in turn into local, largely self-contained communities. People were too concerned about their own survival to worry about what was happening outside their neighbourhoods.

'But in recent decades, Gaia is beginning to relent. Our wizards tell us that carbon dioxide levels and temperatures have been trending downwards. It may still be a long time before climates return to normal, whatever normal might be. It seems that it will involve more rainfall—'

As he spoke there was a peel of thunder. The audience applauded, either at the President's superb timing or at the prospect of impending rain.

'As conditions improve, so the process of disintegration is reversing itself. With the reunification of Tuggeranong, the picture is complete. Our hitherto fractious communities are reforming into districts.

'So, where do we go from here? I think the time has come to consider the next phase in the process of reintegration – the restoration of Canberra as a coherent region.

I have a project in mind that will help with that process.'

***

Crispin's project was, by the standards of his time, an ambitious one. He had often looked out over the enticing gap of some 300 metres between the southern and northern shores of Lake Burley Griffin. One could still see where the once mighty Commonwealth Avenue Bridge had spanned that gap. Centuries of disuse and neglect had seen the bridge reduced to a few pylons sticking forlornly in the mud and stagnant pools.

The communities of Canberra would supply one hundred thick wooden poles to be set across the divide in pairs, six metres apart and six metres from the next pair. Crossbeams and planking would then be added to create a new bridge to reunite north and south, to facilitate trade between the districts.

The survey party that marked out where the pylons would be laid was a team of economists from Anu. They were ignorant of the principles of surveying, but so was practically everyone else in Canberra. But they could do sums and they were used to mucking about in fish ponds.

The poles were obtained, but who was going to have the difficult and dirty job of driving them into the mud? On the northern side, it would be done by the hitherto infamous Belco Beastly Boys, that ungallant band of incompetents that had so miserably failed in their efforts to invade North Canberra. They were under the watchful eyes of Lieutenant Shrubsole and Sergeant Owwible.

As they worked, they sang their song:
With great big ropes, we raise up lots of poles
With hammer blows, we drive them into holes
On the southern side, the task of hammering the poles was given to the Brindabella Brigands and several former feudal lords. They were led by the Count of Condor and a man with a bristling ginger moustache and a bullet-shaped head.

Whenever a pole was raised into position, the Baron would shout, 'Give me Thor.' The Count would struggle to pass a huge hammer to him. The Baron would shout 'Hit them with your sledge hammer' as he drove the poles into the mud. Each pole he hammered was someone he hated: his incompetent Beastly Boys, his gormless Brindabella Brigands, the Tyrant of Turner, Trex Guard, Diana, and worst of all, his sister Beth.

As he unleashed his hatred upon the world, so he released his hatred of it. He became a kinder, more genial man helped, no doubt, by the tender loving care of Helen Hart. Also, he was now achieving something tangible in the world. He saw it as 'his bridge'.

Bit by bit, the structure took shape. It had a bit of a bend in it, because economists were used to thinking in curves. The timbers used, scrounged as they were by enthusiastic local communities from anything resembling a tree, or former part of a tree, were of variable quality.

At last it was complete, and was a wonder to behold. Sure, it creaked and swayed in the wind, and it often had to be repaired. But in symbol and in substance, it linked north and south: Canberra was becoming whole again.

Part Three
Crispin IX

22. Crispin Spalding's Legacy

At the Convocation, few of the delegates had noticed a small boy who sat from time to time in the galleries. He didn't understand much of what was going on, but he knew it was very important because there were so many people there. He was proud that his grandfather was in charge of the proceedings.

The young Crispin watched the first bridge over Burley Griffin in more than a century take shape. He was one of the first to walk on it, hand in hand with his father and grandfather. As bridges go, it was neither straight nor sturdy, but Canberrans were proud of it because it was *their* bridge.

Forty years later, when he became President Crispin IX, he ordered the demolition of that bridge and its replacement with a straighter, bigger and stronger one. Other bridges across Burley Griffin had also been built by then, to cope with the growing volume of traffic between north and south.

The roads on which Canberrans propelled their bicycles or biofuel/solar/electric vehicles were macadamised: not as good as the bitumen roads of their ancestors, but better than the potholed dirt tracks they'd had to endure for over a century. They were also making plans to revive light rail.

Bit by bit, the climate was improving: temperatures were becoming cooler and rainfall was more regular. More trees and crops were planted. Food shortages became a thing of the past. Burley Griffin started to resemble the lake it had been, instead of a series of ponds.

Canberra's population started to grow again. This was due to a more optimistic populace adopting a three-child policy: 'one for mum, one for dad, and one for Canberra'.

***

There were two events that Crispin remembered from his youth that stuck in his memory, even though it would be many years before he realised the significance of them.

At the time of Convocation, his grandfather held a meeting with two men who were known to young Crispin as Uncle Norman and Uncle Cyril. In this case, the term 'uncle' simply meant that he was acquainted with them. He liked Uncle Norman, a cheery fellow who often entertained him with fascinating facts about the natural world. He didn't like Uncle Cyril, who turned up his nose at him and seemed to be a slimy character.

Cyril had laid out a brightly coloured map that young Crispin thought was very pretty, but he couldn't understand it at all. Much of the map was faded, but there were some brightly coloured stars and circles and squares.

'This is a map of the mineral deposits of New South Wales,' said Cyril. 'It's over two hundred years old.'

'The brown symbols are iron deposits,' explained Norman. 'You can see we've got some deposits close by, while there are others a bit further north. There are also deposits of copper and base metals.'

'What are the yellow ones?' asked young Crispin.

Norman grinned. 'Gold.'

There were lots of gold symbols on the map. 'Does that mean we are rich?'

'I'm afraid not,' replied Cyril sourly. 'Most of these deposits would have been mined out long ago.'

'Not necessarily,' Norman replied. 'They would have been abandoned when demand for metals fell during the great economic collapse of the twenty first century. But now, we need those metals. Even low grade ores would be worth extracting.'

Crispin's grandfather took out a ruler and moved it round in a circle based on Canberra. 'So if we were to expand our region to take in all lands within about seventy or eighty kilometres, that should cover at least twenty mineral sites.'

Cyril smiled. 'Those lands are largely uninhabited. It shouldn't be difficult to take them over.'

Norman nodded. 'But we'll have to go a bit further north to get coke.'

***

The second incident from Crispin's youth happened a year or two later. He wasn't pleased that Cyril had installed himself as Presidential advisor. He feared that one day, Cyril might overthrow his grandfather and become President.

Auntie Jezebel and Uncle Quentin also used to visit a lot. He didn't think Cyril liked them until one day when he saw Jezebel and Cyril kissing in a corner of the garden. He told on them to Uncle Quentin, who got very cross.

An ugly scene followed: Cyril finished up with a black eye, while Jezebel had some difficult explaining to do. She told Quentin that she had only done it to insinuate herself with the President's right hand man as part of her plot to get Quentin made President, with herself as First Lady. Quentin was stupid enough to believe her.

The incident was to have important ramifications. Cyril's enemies, who included Norman and the Tyrant of Turner, were then able to move against him, and he was banished to his previous job as advisor to the Governor of Gungahlin. Meanwhile, Quentin and Jezebel were no longer welcome in the capital, except at Advisory Council meetings. They finished up running a duck farm in Queanbeyan.

***

By the time Crispin succeeded his father, Crispin VIII, as President of Canberra, the region had expanded to cover all lands within about 70 to 80 kilometres from the city. The Canberrans did indeed find deposits of gold, copper, iron and other metals. Methods of smelting them were initially crude, until the Wizards of Siro developed some small but surprisingly effective furnaces.

Canberrans had started trading with communities east of the Blue Mountains. They were able to get the bituminous coal that they needed. As long as it was called coke, and smelting took place at secluded locations, nobody complained about the modest amounts of greenhouse gases that were produced.

The three things that Canberrans needed most were metal, plastic and glass to renew their infrastructure and to build new, less ramshackle homes. They now had the metals that they could smelt, while the glassmaking industry had started up again. By delving through old texts, the Wizards of Siro rediscovered the ancient arts of making biofuels and plastics from Safflower seeds.

So, in the reign of Crispin IX, Canberra grew and started to exert its influence over neighbouring regions. It could trade gold, but it turned out it had a far better commodity. The Scholars of Anu and the Wizards of Siro had knowledge – knowledge that other communities craved and for which they were willing to trade produce.

Thus, it was the legacy of Crispin Spalding, the creation of the Black Mountain Trust to keep the flame of knowledge burning at Anu and Siro that proved to be Canberra's greatest asset.

Meanwhile, bit by bit, things started to cool down.

***

On a cold winter's morning, Crispin IX led a hardy band of souls up the track to the lookout on Mount Ainslie.

Amongst his party there were an old man and an old woman. They were surprisingly robust. Alongside them trotted a young boy.

'Are we there yet, Grandpa?' asked the little boy.

'Almost … Yes, here we are.' As he stood on the summit, Trex Guard hoisted his grandson on his shoulders and pointed to the Brindabellas. Diana stood beside him and put her arm round his waist.

'Can you see those white patches on the hills?'

'What are they?' asked the little boy.

'Snow.'

'What's that?'

'Oh, something special. Something that hasn't been seen for a long, long time'

President Crispin IX had tears in his eyes. He knew the story: his illustrious ancestor, Crispin Spalding, had stood on that very spot two centuries earlier and uttered Crispin's Prophecy: 'When next you see snow on the Brindabellas, you will know that Gaia's Curse is being lifted.'

The Age of Global Warming was coming to an end. The human race could get back to doing whatever it had been doing centuries earlier – if anyone could remember what that was – until the next crisis came along.

About the Author

Robert Phillips grew up in Adelaide, where he first started writing for theatre. His full-length science fiction play *Technocraton* was published by Heinemann in 1976.

Moving to Canberra, he became an aviation risk analyst with the Civil Aviation Safety Authority and its predecessors. This inspired him to write *A Risky Life* (Halstead Press, 2014), which describes the risks in life that people are likely to encounter.

He has written several books, plays both long and short, articles, and short stories. His numerous technical papers, which often contained algebra, caused him to be accused of practicing black magic.

Canberraesque was originally written in random order as a series of short stories for a writers' group that met at the ACT Writers Centre, of which he was Secretary for several years. He is also a member of the Canberra Speculative Fiction Guild, which hasn't banned him yet despite his penchant for puns.

A former Convenor of the Downer Community Association, he now lives in retirement with a Burmese cat in the Grand Duchy of North Lyneham.

The author may be contacted via his website:
www.robertphillips.com.au